CW00736264

A
Delight

Mike Peacock

ISBN: 979-8-55-630024-8

Cover Illustration by
Abigail Banks & Rebecca Peacock

For Sophie & Ruby

1

The Beginning

In the beginning, there was a tree...

Actually there were quite a lot of trees, but this one was rather special.

To be honest, in the very beginning there was actually nothing at all. Oh hang on; let's start the story again...

In the beginning, there was nothing... And then God, the Father of all Creation, made everything – stars and planets, land and seas, plants and creatures. And people. Two people to be precise. Called Adam and Eve.

He placed these two people in the middle of a beautiful garden – the most wondrous place in all the earth.

At the centre of which was a particular tree;
that particular tree which I mentioned before.

And God told Adam and Eve that they could do
anything they wanted – anything at all. Only they must
never eat the fruit from the tree.

And that's where the trouble began...

2

Heaven

Heaven. A long, long time later. How much later is difficult to say. That's one of the funny things about Heaven – hours and days and weeks don't seem to really matter at all. There's just a general sort of 'now-ness'. It's like being on the best summer holiday ever, except there are no bedtimes and you never have to go back to school at the end of it.

Heaven is literally the coolest place ever. I don't mean 'cool' as in chilly and cold - the sort of 'cool' where you expect a polar bear to wander around the corner at any minute. Although, to be honest, you probably <u>could</u> find a polar bear in Heaven because... well... in Heaven, you can find pretty much anything.

Anything you can imagine.

And a whole load of things that you haven't even got round to imagining yet.

Yes, Heaven is amazing – let's just leave it at that. It's like having all of the best, and all of the most beautiful, and all of the most fabulous things you could ever think of... all in one place... a place that keeps growing and expanding and getting bigger... and all the time even newer and cooler and even more brilliant things are being designed and invented to fit into all the new space. It's just like that. Heaven is perfect.

Usually...

3

"Gabe!"

Gabe flew through the air. Travelling at a terrific speed, the little angel hurtled across the clear blue canopies of Heaven.

'Yeeehay!' he cried. 'This is *awesome!*'

It had all started so well. He'd taken off from Angel Air Traffic Control and performed every manoeuvre perfectly. He'd flown at just the right speed … at just the right height…

Down below, in the control room, Phin the Senior Training Instructor carefully observed him on a screen.

Gabe was determined that this would be the year when he finally passed his flying test. (It was in fact his seventeenth attempt to pass – although he'd never admit that to the likes of you and me.) At just under a hundred years old Gabe was one of the youngest angels, but it was still a little embarrassing that he hadn't managed to graduate from flight school yet. However, nothing could stop him now…

He swooped over a forest and did a celebratory barrel roll, startling a passing pterodactyl. (I told you that you can find anything in Heaven.)

'Steady as you go, Gabe' muttered the voice of Phin in his ear.

Gabe grinned.

Swooping over a snowy valley, he began his final approach towards the Heavenly Citadel…

'Watch your speed,' muttered Phin.

Almost there, Gabe thought to himself. Just a few more miles to go… a nice neat landing to perform… and at long last, I will have passed this silly test.

'Gabe…' came the warning voice of Phin.

At last, I'll be a fully-fledged official angel, thought Gabe.

No more being bossed about... no more being told what to do... I'll finally *be* someone... I'll–

'*Gabe!*' shouted Phin.

With a jolt, Gabe jerked back to reality - and realised that he was now heading towards the Citadel at an incredibly high speed. Up ahead, he could see its high towers glinting in the sunlight. Approaching... approaching rather quickly... approaching much, much *too* quickly...

'*Gabe, pull up!*' yelled Phin.

Down in the Angel Air Traffic Control Centre, warning lights began to flash. Phin sighed.

The towers now loomed larger and larger. Gabe could see the faces of people within, who were beginning to look up and stare out of the windows.

They didn't seem pleased to see him. Desperately, he tried to change direction, tilting and adjusting his wings.

But they wouldn't respond...

In the Angel Air Traffic Control Centre, a siren began to wail.

All the other flight control angels stopped what they were doing and began to cluster around the main screen...

Up in the air, Gabe strained... and heaved... Desperate to turn... desperate to gain more height... Basically desperate to avoid having an almighty crash with the tower which was now ridiculously close.

'Come on,' he urged himself. 'Come on.' He gave one last desperate heave of his wings.

'Come oooooooon!'

In the Control Centre, there was a hush as dozens of pairs of eyes stared at the dot hurtling across the screen.

'Come on...' breathed Phin.

Wooooosh!

At the last possible moment, Gabe managed to tilt his wings - swerving around the edge of the tower... skimming the bricks... rattling the windows... and causing several angels inside to faint.

In the Control Centre, cheers erupted as everyone applauded and slapped each other on the back. (Almost as if they'd been the ones who'd done all the hard work). Phin collapsed into a chair.

Gabe grinned.

However, back in the Angel Air Traffic Control Centre, warning lights began flashing again...

Gabe stopped grinning. He was still going far too fast. And, with the sudden manoeuvre around the tower, he seemed to have lost control of his steering too - and was now heading right towards the heart of the Heavenly City.

In the Angel Air Traffic Control Centre, angels began to rush around in panic. Phin groaned.

Out of control, Gabe hurtled above the streets of the city. He *whooshed* over the heads of a group of former American presidents, who were busy playing badminton in a park (knocking Abraham Lincoln's famous top hat right off his head in the process).

He *rattled* past a table full of senior angels, who were meeting to discuss world peace, scattering their papers all over the floor.

He *spun* past Michelangelo, the famous artist, sending his paints flying all over the lawn, and almost ruining the new portrait of Queen Elizabeth that he'd been working on. Michelangelo shook his fist.

Gabe *buzzed* past a restaurant, where a famous chef was just about to serve his latest creation, forcing the famous chef to fall face-first into his dish (which fortunately turned out to be delicious, so he wasn't too upset.)

Finally, with a mighty effort, straining his wings, Gabe managed to regain control, and steered himself back towards Angel Air Traffic Control.

Everyone in the centre breathed a sigh of relief - until they realised that Gabe was now headed directly towards *them*. They began to panic. Phin put her head in her hands.

Flapping his wings, Gabe frantically tried to slow down.

In the control room, angels scattered in all directions... tripping over each other as they desperately dived for cover.

'*Look out...!*' Gabe cried.

He arrived. There was an almighty:

Crash!

Followed by a:

Rattle!

And then something that went a bit like:

Ker-doiing-a-doiing-a-doiing!

And finally, an...

'Ouch.'

———

4

'The Event'

A short while later, Gabe was sitting propped up in a chair in a corner of the Angel Air Traffic Control room. His uniform was singed... his wings were slightly dented... his helmet was scratched... and his mood was definitely down-in-the-dumps.

The other angels who worked in the control room had dusted themselves off by now and were busy trying to get back to normal.

Some of them frowned in his direction. One of them had a fresh bandage.

'What are we going to do with you, Gabe?' said Phin.

She was sitting opposite her dazed apprentice, nursing a mug of steaming hot chocolate. (By the way, if you've never tasted Heaven's hot chocolate, you really should – it's amazing.)

'Sorry,' said Gabe.

The older angel sighed. The problem was that this was not Gabe's first crash-landing. Or indeed his second. Or his fourteenth for that matter.

'What are we going to do with you?' she said again.

'Give me one more chance,' pleaded Gabe. 'I know what went wrong. I just know that I can be a really great flyer.'

'The thing is, Gabe,' replied Phin. 'You don't need to be a *great* flyer – just a safe one.'

At that moment, as if the emphasise the point, a grumpy-looking angel passed them by holding an icepack to a bruise on his head...

'Gabe,' said Phin, 'You are training to be part of the Angelic Messenger Corp, and one of the most important aspects of that role is the ability to get from one place to another safely.'

Gabe looked at the floor.

'But I'm not even sure I want to be a messenger,' he said. 'I'd much rather be something cool... like... a warrior angel... or maybe I could get a job in development - creating new worlds... or maybe I could even become a guardian angel one day.'

An angel with an eye patch looked across.

'A guardian angel? You?' he snorted.

Phin sighed again. This was not the first time that they had had this sort of conversation. Or indeed the second. She had been Gabe's mentor for the last fifty years, and it had not been entirely... well... straightforward. It wasn't that Gabe was actually <u>bad</u> at things – and you certainly couldn't fault him for enthusiasm - it was just that he wasn't always... very <u>good</u> at anything.

Choir had been a disaster...

(It wasn't that Gabe couldn't sing, it was just that he sang in all the wrong places.)

He'd been kicked out of the design department...

(Since his drawing of an idea for a new spider had caused half the other angels to faint.)

And he wasn't allowed anywhere near the army...

(Certainly not since that infamous incident involving juggling swords and a certain general's toe.)

Phin looked across at Gabe kindly.

'Let's just try and get the hang of the basics first, eh?' she said. 'I'll arrange for another opportunity for you to take the flying test. There's sure to be another slot available in about ten years or so.'

'Ten years!' exclaimed Gabe. 'I can't wait that long.'

'I'm afraid you're going to have to' said Phin, 'there is rather a lot going on in Heaven at the moment.'

She leaned forwards.

'What with 'The Event' going on, and all that,' she added, tapping the side of her nose conspiratorially.

Ah yes, 'The Event'...

Gabe knew all about that. 'The Event' was in fact the worst kept secret in Heaven. Everyone had been talking it about since the dawn of time, and that whole unfortunate business with the tree.

'The Event' was God's Great Plan to put the universe back in order... to rid the world of all that was bad and wrong and simply not right... and restore creation to its former glory.

The precise details were top, top secret. But the whole of Heaven was bursting with excitement about it, and everyone seemed to have an important role to play. Everyone, that is, except Gabe.

Phin stood up.

'Don't worry, ten years will fly by,' she said patting Gabe on the shoulder. 'You'll see.'

At that moment there came a sound.

How can I describe it? Perhaps if you imagined the best choir in the world doing an impression of a train... going backwards... underwater... whilst playing electric guitars... (but sounding really good) … it would be a bit like that.

It was certainly a very important sound. As soon as they heard it, every angel in the control room stopped what they were doing and hurriedly gathered around the central message screen. Phin rushed over to join them.

She frowned as she read the message and looked over at Gabe.

'What is it?' he asked.

'It appears,' Phin replied slowly, 'that you and I have been summoned to the Throne Room.'

Gabe's jaw dropped.

'What?!' he exclaimed. '*The* Throne Room? As in the Throne Room of the Lord God Almighty himself? The King of kings? The Lord of lords?'

'Yes,' said Phin.

'We've been summoned *there*?'

'Yes.'

'You and me? Both of us? At the same time?'

Yes!'

'Oh… wow...' Gab marvelled. 'I wonder why...'

And then a thought struck him.

'Oh, no! You don't think He's heard about the crash, do you? I'm not going to get into trouble, am I?'

'I have absolutely no idea,' said Phin, straightening up her uniform and heading towards the door. 'However, what I do know is that we'll be in hot water if we keep Him waiting. Come along!'

5

The Tree

The tree...

Remember the tree?

The tree right at the beginning of everything...

The tree that had stood in the middle of the Garden of Eden... and led to all those problems...

It had seemed like such a good idea...

God had created Adam and Eve – the first ever people – and given them the garden - a wonderful, beautiful place where they could live in perfect harmony with their Creator...

But, you see – and here's the really important thing - God had wanted them to be his <u>friends</u>.

(Not servants. Or people who were simply being nice to him because they had to.)

Friends...

And so that meant Adam and Eve had to be free to choose...

To be with God... to be his friends...

To live their lives His way...

Or not...

And so the tree was planted.

The Tree of the Knowledge of Good and Evil.

Adam and Eve were given one simple rule: they must never, ever eat the fruit from that tree.

That would be the test...

And by them choosing to follow that rule, God would know whether they were willing to live his way... Or not...

It was a great idea!

And it worked really well at first...

Until, one day, when God's enemy arrived in the garden... and decided to cause some mischief...

6

The Throne Room

The corridors leading to the Throne Room were bustling. Dozens of angels were hurrying and scurrying... backwards and forwards... up and down stairs... in and out of meeting rooms.

There were angels of every shape and size you could imagine - junior angels, senior angels, mighty archangels, enormous seraphim and tiny cherubim. It was a hive of activity. Everyone busy; everyone getting ready for '*The Event*'.

'Won't be long now,' whispered Phin.

Gabe stared at everything, wide-eyed, in amazement.

Through one doorway he caught a glimpse of a map of the earth, showing the position of all the different angelic forces (before it was quickly closed by a stern-looking commander.)

On a stairwell, he passed groups of angels carrying folders marked 'Top Secret' and 'Archangel Eyes Only' and talking in whispered voices (and going even quieter as Gabe walked by.)

In the main hallway, they suddenly had to jump to one side as a pair of tough-looking warrior angels lumbered heavily down the corridor in the opposite direction, great swords strapped to their backs.

It was all terribly exciting.

Finally, Gabe and Phin arrived at an enormous pair of doors - the entrance to the Throne Room...

Imagine, if you can, the biggest door you've ever seen. Now times it by a hundred... (and add 12)... They were about that size. And standing in front of them was an enormous angel.

This wasn't your pretty, Christmas card sort of angel that likes to spend its spare time playing the harp. This was Michael, the Great Warrior angel –

commander of the armies of the Heavenly Host (known as Mikey to his friends). He towered over the other angels who were bustling around the corridors. His amour gleamed. Although, if you looked carefully, you could see scratches and dents from the numerous battles he'd fought over the centuries. His muscles bulged. His great arms bore the names of demons he'd defeated in battle tattooed across them. He wore an enormous sword strapped across his back and a permanent scowl on his face.

'Yes?' he demanded.

Gabe gulped.

'We… er… have an appointment,' stammered Phin.

The massive archangel looked them over for a moment... grunted… and then stepped to the side.

'Enter,' he rumbled.

The massive doors to the Throne Room swung open…

There's really no way to describe the Heavenly Throne Room. So I won't. It's indescribable.

Well, okay I'll give it a go...

Imagine, if you can, the most impressive royal palace ever built... with gold and silver furniture... plush carpets... enormous columns... high ceilings...

Have you done that? Good. Now imagine it being a hundred times more grand. Actually, make it a thousand times.

Imagine the walls decorated with the most magnificent rainbows and sunsets that have ever been seen... the ceiling lit by the most beautiful stars in the universe... Imagine, in the background, the sound of heavenly choirs and musicians playing on the most wonderful instruments, the most wondrous music that has ever been heard...

Can you imagine all that? Don't worry if you can't – I told you it's indescribable.

Nervously, Gabe and Phin made their way down the central aisle, followed closely by the great bulk of the archangel Mikey. The room must have been at least a hundred miles long, and possibly a hundred miles wide too. And yet, it seemed only to take them moments to reach the far end and the foot of the steps that led up to the Great Throne itself. If the room was hard to describe, then the throne is even harder…

It was, in fact, not one throne but three - three separate thrones, yet woven together as if to make one. Like three separate shapes that have been drawn on a piece of paper overlapping each other - distinct and different, yet merging into one.

They had been lovingly carved and decorated with every precious stone and jewel imaginable. (And quite a few that aren't imaginable yet – owing to the fact that God keeps creating new ones.) They shone and shimmered with the brightness of a thousand suns, which you would have thought would make them hard to look at - and yet for some reason, they weren't.

They were… well… they were indescribable.

Next to them, on either side towered two mighty archangels, each almost as tall as Mikey. These weren't warriors though. They seemed as old as time itself yet, in their eyes, twinkled a childlike curiosity. In their hands, they each held an ancient book and were carefully recording all that was said and done – not only in the Throne Room but in all of creation too.

On the central throne, sat God the Father.

He spoke…

The voice of the Father was like a beautiful song - a sound as big as the universe... and yet gentle as a whisper... it filled you up 'til you wanted to burst and left you feeling tingly all over for days...

'Ah, Gabe…' it said. 'Thank you so much for coming to see us.'

Gabe shuffled nervously.

'We have been keeping an eye on you, young Gabriel,' continued the voice of the Father.

Phin stepped forwards.

'I am so sorry about that, your honour,' she burst out. 'It's not his fault... just high spirits... I'm sure that if I keep a closer eye on him...'

'Indeed,' said the voice of the Father, with just a hint of gentle firmness in His voice (the sort of hint that implies it would be a good idea to stop talking now).

Phin fell silent, staring at her feet.

'Now then,' the voice of the Father went on, turning his attention back to Gabe. 'I have given this matter a lot of thought, and it seems to me that the best thing I can do with you… is to give you a job.'

Gabe was gob-smacked.

'A *job*?' he gasped. 'For me?'

'You are training to be a messenger, are you not?'

'Well, yes,' stammered Gabe.

'Good. Then you shall deliver a message.'

Gabe's mind was in a whirl. Phin raised her hand questioningly, but the voice of the Father continued:

'You are to travel down to Earth... to the country of Israel... the region of Galilee... where you will find a young girl called Mary. And you are to tell her that she is going to have a baby.'

'A baby?' asked Gabe.

'Yes,' said the Father.

Gabe was puzzled.

'Oh... okay... I mean I don't mean to be funny, but... don't people have babies all the time? And I'm pretty sure they don't normally need an angel to come and tell them about it...'

'That is true,' said the Father with a smile. 'However, this is no ordinary baby. His name shall be Jesus, and...'

He paused for a moment, to let the significance of what he was about to say sink in...

'He will be my Son.'

Gabe's jaw dropped. He glanced at Phin, who seemed just as stunned.

As did Mikey. As did the two archangels at the sides of the throne for that matter.

'Your Son?' gasped Gabe.

'Yes,' said the Father. 'Through this child, I am going to restore the whole of my creation. I am going to put everything back to the way it was meant to be in the very beginning. Ever since that whole unfortunate business with the tree, there has been so much heartache... so much hurt... and struggle. Human beings have squabbled... and argued... and fought amongst themselves ever since...

But now, through this child, I shall make a way for the world to be healed again! Where there has been war... there will be peace; where there has been sadness... there will be joy; where there has been doubt... there will be hope. And everyone - every single person - will have the chance to be my friends once more!'

There was silence in the Throne room. Gabe looked to Phin... who looked to Mikey... who looked to the two archangels next to the throne… who were looking at each other in amazement.

'So... this is part of The Event?' asked Gabe.

'This is the <u>whole</u> of The Event,' replied the Father. 'The message you are delivering will be the starting point for the most important event in the whole of history.'

Gabe was stunned.

'Er...' Phin attempted to find her voice.

'Yes, Phin?'

'The thing is, your majesty... your supremeness... your most holiest and highest... the thing is...'

'Yes?'

'This is *Gabe* you're sending. And he can be a bit... well, you know...'

'I know.'

'But he's...'

There was a rumble from the throne.

'Are you assuming that I haven't thought this through properly?' said the Father.

Phin blushed... and made a sort of strangled noise in her throat... and then stared at the floor as if willing it to open up and swallow her.

'However,' said the voice of the Father. 'I do note your concern. And that's why I'm not sending him alone.'

'You're not?' said Phin.

'No. You can go along too and keep an eye on him. If you don't mind.'

'Yes... I mean no... I mean yes, of course,' blustered Phin.

Behind them, Mikey sniggered.

'Oh, and Michael?' the Father added. 'It might be a good idea if you go along too...'

7

"I don't believe it!"

'I don't believe it,' thundered Mikey.

He was pacing up and down in a small court-yard, just outside the Throne Room. It was theoretical-ly outside of God's hearing. (Although, to be honest, nowhere is outside of God's hearing - as he's techni-cally everywhere and knows everything that's going on anyway. But sometimes it makes you feel better.)

'I don't believe it,' Mikey bellowed again.

'It does seem rather incredible,' admitted Phin, who was leaning against a nearby column for support.

It was rather a posh courtyard - with statues, pretty fountains and those cleverly designed little shrubs tastefully arranged around the edges.

Gabe didn't notice the shrubs. He was sitting on the floor, his head reeling from the events of the last few minutes. Plus he was rather keen to keep out of Mikey's way.

'Fancy sending someone untrained and inexperienced on an important mission like this,' continued Mikey. 'A trainee, and a... and a...'

He looked at Phin, trying to decide on the right word.

'Teacher?' suggested Phin.

'Exactly!' he snapped, then stormed off, and began pacing on the far side of the courtyard.

Gabe was stunned. His mind was spinning with questions, like: How in Heaven had this happened? Why had God chosen him? Was it all some sort of mistake? But then, that was impossible - God never makes mistakes. Perhaps it's some sort of test...

And why...? (And this was the really big question – the one that he kept on circling back to...)

'Why a baby?' he asked out loud.

Phin looked across.

'Why send a baby?' asked Gabe again.

'I mean if you're going to save the world, wouldn't it be better to send an army... or some great hero... or something... I mean... what can a *baby* do?'

'Er...' began Phin, and then stopped.

'Er…' she began again. 'I'm sure that it will all become clear in good time.'

'But it doesn't make sense.'

'Maybe not to the likes of you and me, but obviously God knows what he's doing. Our job is simply to do what we've been asked to do - even if we don't entirely understand it...'

Gabe shrugged.

'I suppose,' he said.

'Now then,' said Phin, holding out a hand and hauling Gabe to his feet. 'We need to start making preparations – we've got quite the journey ahead of us. You've not been down to the Earth before – you never know, it might be fun.'

'It will not be fun,' bellowed Mikey as he strode back towards them from the other side of the courtyard. 'This is a military operation - and it will be run as such. There will be no sightseeing, no dilly-dally-ing, and no larking about. Is that understood?'

'Someone's going to be good company,' muttered Phin.

'Listen to me,' growled Mikey, 'this is a serious mission – upon which hangs the fate of the universe. Your job is to do <u>exactly</u> what I tell you.'

Gabe raised a hand nervously.

'Actually,' he said, 'this is technically <u>my</u> mission. You were both just sent along to help me out.'

Mikey rounded on him. 'Oh really?' he said. 'And I suppose you know all about planet Earth and the dangers that might be waiting for us down below?'

'Now, now...' said Phin, stepping in between them. 'This has been a big surprise for us all, but I'm sure God has got everything under control. Now, I suggest we all go off and get ourselves ready for the big journey.'

Mikey huffed, then stormed away.

Phin turned back to Gabe.

'Don't worry about him,' she said.

'What did he mean about dangers?' Asked Gabe. 'I didn't think anything on Earth could be dangerous to an angel.'

Phin hesitated for a second.

'I wouldn't trouble yourself about that,' she said lightly. 'Besides we're hardly going to be down there long enough for anything bad to happen. Now, come along! I want to find out if they've invented peppermint down there yet. I do find it hard to keep track of the order that things happen in...'

She headed off. Gabe trailed behind her...

8

The Tree

The tree...

The famous tree...

Of the Knowledge of Good and Evil, stood strong and tall in the middle of the Garden of Eden, whilst Adam and Eve played happily nearby.

But God's enemy was watching...

His name was Lucifer, and he was cunning and sly, and as slippery as a snake.

He realised that if he could get Adam and Eve to break the rule – the rule to not eat the fruit from the tree – that it would ruin their relationship with God... and cause a whole world of trouble... (He liked that idea...)

But the trouble was, there was no way that he could ever _force_ Adam and Eve to eat the fruit.

Although...

Although he could <u>persuade</u> them to ...

So Lucifer watched, and he waited and he bided his time - looking for an opportunity.

Until one day it came...

One afternoon, he found Eve playing by herself near the tree. Lucifer approached, disguised as a snake...

(I told you he was slippery)

'Hmmm. That fruit looks so good,' he said.

'Yes, it really does,' she replied, staring wistfully at the delicious-looking tree. 'But we're not allowed to touch it.'

'Are you sure about that?' asked Lucifer.

And so...

With many cunning words and many crafty questions - he began to charm... and convince... and persuade her that perhaps she'd misunderstood God's instructions about the tree. That perhaps the fruit was okay to eat after all...

And, before long...

She believed him...

And Adam and Eve found themselves breaking God's one and only rule...

And that's when a whole world of trouble began...

9

Earth

Planet Earth...

In a town called Nazareth, in the region of Galilee, in the country of Israel – there was a noise. It went a bit like this:

Phffzzplop!

No, I'm not being rude. It was in fact the sound of Phin arriving on the planet's surface. She looked around, blinking in the bright afternoon sunlight. She appeared to be in an empty courtyard... at the back of a row of houses... surrounded by rows of drying washing. There was no one around.

'Mikey!' she hissed.

A head popped up from behind a nearby wall. It was Mikey's. (Don't worry - the rest of him was there too; it was just that it was hidden behind the wall and you couldn't see it yet.)

'Here,' he said.

Mikey scrambled over the wall and advanced across the courtyard towards where Phin was standing. (You see, I told you he was okay).

'Area secure,' he announced, gruffly.

'Jolly good,' replied Phin. 'Er, where's Gabe?'

They looked around. A quick scan of the area revealed that - other than the two of them – the courtyard was remarkably angel-free. Phin groaned.

Mikey opened his mouth and then closed it again. He had the look on his face of someone who has been about to say 'Whose idea was it to bring that idiot along?' but then has suddenly remembered whose idea it <u>had</u> actually been.

'I suppose we'd better go and find him,' sighed Phin.

They didn't get far.

'Fflflbnyputt!'

It was a strange noise; a muffled, garbled sort of cry – the sort of sound you get if you try talking to someone who has crawled all the way underneath their duvet and can't find the way out again. (You know the one.) Mikey and Phin glanced at one other.

'What was that?' whispered Phin.

The noise came again.

'Hararyjniopcupf!'

Now they were alarmed.

'I'm not sure,' admitted Mikey, 'but it doesn't sound particularly happy.' They looked around the area of the courtyard, trying to figure out where the noise was coming from. Other than themselves and the piles of washing, there was nothing to be seen.

'Fzdfadt! kfldogap!'

Now the noise was getting louder. Whatever it was, it was definitely sounding more and more upset.

'I think it's coming from the far corner,' hissed Phin.

They both looked towards the corner, where lay an especially large pile of washing. It began to shake.

'Shisf... ahbxnzis... ddtfkkagpo...!'

Cautiously, the two angels began to advance towards it.

'What *is* it?' whimpered Phin. 'Some sort of Earth monster? Has it eaten Gabe?'

The mound began to shudder... and tremble...

Mikey drew his sword... Phin cowered behind him... Suddenly, the pile reared up and lurched forward...

Phin screamed...

The creature roared...

*'Shufapdklu...*waaaaitaminute – *it's me!'*

A sheet fell off its head.

'Gabe?' gasped Phin.

It was indeed Gabe.

And not some sort of monster, you'll be relieved to know. With difficulty, Gabe struggled out from underneath the remainder of the giant washing pile and stood facing the other two. Phin breathed a sigh of relief. Mikey simply tutted and put his sword away (looking slightly disappointed that he hadn't been able to use it.)

'Gabe,' demanded Phin, 'why in Heaven's name are you pretending to be a monster?'

'I wasn't,' said Gabe. 'I just... sort of crash-landed into the washing basket and... got myself a bit tangled up...'

'Well, you gave us all quite the fright,' reprimanded Phin.

'Speak for yourself,' muttered Mikey.

'Sorry,' said Gabe.

Phin held out a hand and helped Gabe clamber out of the remains of the – now slightly battered – washing basket.

'When you two have finished messing about,' said Mikey, 'you can get this place tidied up. I'm going to check the perimeter; make sure everything's secure.'

He stalked off out of the courtyard. Phin surveyed the washing that was now strewn across the ground.

'He's right, you know,' she said. 'We're not even supposed to be seen by anyone. We can't leave all this mess lying about. Come on.'

Carefully, they began to tidy and fold the clean sheets back into neat piles. Although, to be honest, it was mostly Phin doing the work - Gabe was too busy looking around.

'So, this is Earth?' he said.

'Yes.'

Gabe stared at the houses lining the courtyard... he gazed at the trees in the field beyond... and the mountains in the distance...

'Phin?' he asked after a moment.

'Hmmm?' said the older angel, still busy trying to tidy up.

'Are you sure we're in the right place?'

Phin looked up.

'Of course we are,' she said. 'These are the precise coordinates that we were given for finding Mary.'

'Right.'

Gabe hesitated.

'It's just that...'

'What?'

'This is supposed to be a big deal - the greatest event in history... the start of God's Great Plan... and this Mary is supposed to be this amazing person who's been chosen to be right at the heart of it all...'

'Yes? Your point is?'

'Well, shouldn't we be looking somewhere a bit more special? After all, Mary's really important. She's bound to be a queen... or at least a great leader... or something... We should be looking in castles... or palaces... places like that... Not mucking about amongst the washing in someone's backyard in the middle of nowhere.'

Phin opened her mouth to reply, but just at that moment, Mikey's head appeared over a nearby wall. (Don't worry; the rest of him was still there – just out of sight again.)

'Incoming!' he yelled.

'Pardon me?' said Gabe

'It means that someone's coming,' said Phin. 'Now quickly; let's get ourselves out of sight.'

Swiftly, the angels scrambled into different hiding places. Mikey disappeared behind the wall... Phin climbed a tree... and Gabe threw the sheet back over his head again.

Footsteps approached...

10

Mary

A girl walked into the courtyard. (Or maybe a young lady would be a more accurate way of describing her.) She had a spring in her step and a gentle grace about her that seemed to make the whole world light up. She picked up an empty basket and began to gather in the washing, whilst singing a happy little tune to herself.

After a few moments, a man's voice drifted across from the house nearby.

'Mary!'

The girl turned.

'Mary,' called the voice again. 'Your dinner's almost ready!'

'Won't be long, Papa,' she called back.

She smiled to herself. Then quickly finished filling up her basket, turned and ran toward the house.

The courtyard was empty for a moment. Then one by one, Gabe, Mikey and Phin emerged from their hiding places and gathered in the middle.

'*That's* Mary?' said Gabe.

'Well, yes,' said Phin.

'That's *Mary…*' Gabe said again.

'Well obviously it is,' said Mikey. ' What's the matter? What were you expecting? A sign over her head saying the 'Chosen One'?'

'Well… I… dunno…' Gabe muttered.

Mikey chuckled.

Phin put a hand on her young apprentice's shoulder.

'Don't worry,' she said, 'things aren't always the way they appear. God tends not to look at things in the same way as others. He doesn't judge by what's on the outside. He looks within, into a person's heart. That's where the real treasure is found.'

'Now,' she added. 'I'm sure Mary will be back before too long, and when she is, you can deliver your message - and then we can all pop back home.'

She began fussing around Gabe, brushing dust from his uniform, and generally acting like a proud parent on their child's first day of school.

'This is such a big moment for you,' she said.

Any minute now she's going to spit on a hankie and start trying to wash my face, thought Gabe.

'Now, just relax and try to enjoy it,' she said. 'And don't worry about everybody else.'

'Everybody else?' said Gabe.

'Er, yes,' she said. 'You know, the other angels in Heaven. This is a big moment. Everyone is going to be watching.'

'So don't make a mess of it,' growled Mikey.

Now Gabe felt worried. Phin and Mikey began to walk back to their hiding places.

'Wait a minute,' he called after them.

'Where are you going?'

Phin turned back.

'Well,' she said, 'we can't have all three of us appearing to Mary at once – it would be far too over-whelming for the poor girl. Anyway, this is <u>your</u> moment – enjoy it!'

They disappeared out of sight. Gabe was now all alone in the middle of the courtyard.

'Terrific,' he said.

He looked towards the house where Mary had gone and tried to psyche himself up.

Okay, he thought to himself, this is my big moment. I can do this.

Then a thought struck him.

What am I going to say?

He hadn't actually thought about that. He'd just assumed that it would come to him in the moment. But now that the moment was here – and everyone in Heaven was watching – expecting him to say something really clever…

He paced up and down.

Okay, he thought, how about this:

Mary, how do you feel about becoming incredibly famous?

No, no that wouldn't do...

How about:

Mary, do you believe in angels? Because... I am one!

Er, no. Perhaps not...

How about:

Mary, how do you feel about surprises?

Oh dear...

'Incoming!'

Mikey suddenly yelled from behind the wall.

'Oh, no I'm not ready yet!' squealed Gabe.

He looked around and saw the door of the house opening... he heard the sound of Mary's voice...

In desperation, he ran back to the pile of washing in the corner and dived into it, throwing a sheet over his head.

'What are you doing?!' hissed Phin, from her own hiding place.

Mary entered the courtyard. Still singing the same little song as before, she began to gather the remainder of the washing. She approached the sheet where Gabe was hiding… he squeezed his eyes closed in the hope that this would somehow help him stay hidden…

It didn't.

Mary picked up the sheet.

'Hello,' said Gabe.

Mary stepped backwards in surprise.

'Hello...?' she said.

Gabe stood up and took a deep breath. This was it. This was his big moment. These were the words that would be remembered for all time.

He began:

'I am the Gabeel Ange...'

Oh no. Panic gripped him. His tongue suddenly felt too big to fit into his mouth.

He tried again:

'I am the Angebel Garb...' he stammered.

He could now feel his cheeks glowing red with embarrassment. Behind the wall, he could hear Mikey sniggering.

'Just relax, Gabe,' whispered Phin.

One last try...

'I have been sent to tell you baby that a Mary is going to have me!' he blurted out.

Mikey was now almost choking as he tried to stifle his laughter. Gabe stared desperately at Mary.

'I'm afraid I'm really not quite following you,' she said. 'Why don't you take a deep breath and start again. I find that always helps me when I feel nervous about something.'

Gabe did. Then he took a few more.

'I'm sorry,' he said. 'I'm supposed to be delivering you this really important message and... I'm making a mess of it...'

Mary put a reassuring hand on his arm.

'You're doing just fine,' she said. 'Perhaps if you stepped out of the washing basket it would make the message seem more impressive. Here, come and sit by me.'

She sat down on a stone wall nearby and patted the place next to her. Gabe trudged over and sat.

'It's my first day,' he mumbled.

'And I think you're doing very well,' encouraged Mary. 'Things are always difficult the first time you try them. Did you break my washing basket, by the way?

'Sorry about that,' mumbled Gabe.

'Never mind,' said Mary. 'Why don't we start again? Whom did you say you are?'

'Gabriel. The Angel Gabriel. Although everyone just calls me Gabe.'

'An angel? Really? A proper one?'

'Yes. Well, sort of... not quite a proper one. I haven't passed my flight test yet... so I'm not official. But please don't tell anyone about that...'

He trailed off, miserably.

'I won't,' she promised. 'You know, this is very exciting for me. I've never met an angel before.'

Gabe grunted and looked at the floor.

'You were saying something about a message?' she prompted.

'Yes, yes...'

He drew himself together...

'Mary, I have got a very important message for you. You have been specially selected for an incredibly important task.'

She nodded encouragingly.

'Go on.'

'The thing is, God is going to send his very own Son to Earth, and he's chosen you out of every single person on the planet throughout the whole of history – er, the girls, that is - to be his mother!'

Gabe looked at her expectantly. Mary sat back.

'Wow...' she breathed.

'Any questions?'

'One or two,' admitted Mary.

'Ah…'

'For example… how will this be?'

Gabe hesitated. This was not a question that he had been expecting.

'Yes, well that's rather complicated...' he began.

'Thought it might be.'

'Er… Well… You know how the universe was created in the beginning?'

'No.'

'Okay, let me try another way: do you know how the basic principles of pan-dimensional physics work?'

'No.'

'Oh… Quantum chemical synergy?'

'Sorry,' admitted Mary, 'I've no idea what you're talking about.'

Gabe was frustrated.

'The thing is,' said Gabe, 'God is going to do

something really amazing - but I've absolutely no idea how to explain it to you.'

'Oh, you mean it's a miracle?' said Mary.

'Er... yes!'

'Oh, that's so much easier to understand!' she said.

'It is?'

'Of course.'

Gabe grinned with relief.

'So, you're okay to do it?' he asked. 'You're happy to be the mother of the Son of God? Because you can say 'no'... although it'd make everything a lot easier if you said yes...'

Mary smiled.

'Yes,' she said. 'I would be honoured. I would be honoured to do whatever the Lord asks of me.'

Gabe leapt out of his seat.

'*Yes!*' he cried.

11

"We have a problem…"

It was a few minutes later…

Mary had returned back inside the house. Mikey and Phin had emerged from where they'd been hiding, and they were now standing gathered around Gabe in the middle of the now-empty courtyard. Phin clapped her hands together.

'Well done!' she cried. 'You did it! Your first assignment! Message delivered, mission accomplished!'

She beamed with pride at her young apprentice. Gabe blushed.

'I suppose you did get there in the end,' Mikey grunted, clapping him on the shoulder (and almost knocking Gabe over in the process).

'I did, didn't I?' grinned Gabe.

'So...er... what happens now?' he added.

'We go home,' said Phin. 'That's it... job done. God's Great Plan - The Event - is now well and truly underway. Mary will have her baby... the baby will grow up to do... whatever it is he's going to do... and creation will be restored. The important thing is that we've played our part. And now, it's time for us to head back home... put our feet up... and have a well-earned hot chocolate.'

The idea of the hot chocolate was very appealing. However, before the angels could get any further, there came a shout - very loud and from within the house. It went like this:

'What?!'

It was followed by a lot more words... all of them equally loud... and none of them sounding particularly happy. Then came the sound of a door being slammed at the front of the house.

The angels glanced at each other. Then they

quickly ran and peered around the corner to try and see

what was going on.

A young man - the one with the loud, angry words – was storming down the garden path. He was closely followed by Mary.

'It's okay, Joseph,' she was saying.

He stopped and turned.

'Okay?' he cried. 'Okay? What part of 'I'm going to have a baby' is okay?'

'But it was an angel who told me,' she pleaded.

'An angel?'

'Yes.'

'Really?'

'Honestly.'

'Oh. That makes it all right then.'

'Does it?' she asked.

'*No!*' he shouted - and stormed off down the road. With a sob, Mary turned and ran back into the house.

'Heaven,' said Phin slowly, 'I think we may have a problem...'

12

What Now?

'What's the problem?' asked Gabe.

The three angels were now sitting on the roof of Mary's house. From down below, they could hear the sounds of arguing... doors slamming... and Mary crying.

'Joseph doesn't believe Mary,' replied Phin. 'And now he's threatening to cancel the wedding.'

'But why?' asked Gabe.

Mikey and Phin glanced at one another.

'Because...' began Phin awkwardly, 'because... he knows that the baby is...you know....'

'What?' asked Gabe.

'You know…'

'What?'

'You know!' snapped Mikey.

'What?!' yelled Gabe, in exasperation.

'Not his!' said Phin.

'Oh...'

Gabe fell silent.

'Joseph thinks that Mary's lying to him,' continued Phin. 'He thinks she must have a... a different boyfriend... and... and now he wants nothing more to do with her...'

'But that's awful,' said Gabe.

'The thing is,' said Phin, 'if Mary doesn't get married... and then the Son of God is born... well... it'll cause quite a scandal.'

'Especially in this age. And in this culture,' added Mikey.

'It will certainly not be particularly helpful with regard to carrying out God's Great Plan,' said Phin. 'There's nothing for it: they simply *must* get married.'

'So what do we do?' asked Gabe.

Mikey flexed his muscles

'I think it's time to pay Joseph a visit,' he said.

'And convince him once and for all that angels are real...'

13

Joseph

Night fell...

It was quite a beautiful night by earth's standards – stars twinkling, half the Milky Way on display... But for the angels gathered on the roof of Joseph's house, there wasn't much time to sit around appreciating the splendour of it all.

'Is this the one?' asked Phin.

'Yeah,' said Mikey. 'Saw him come in about half an hour ago. Plus the crowd outside chanting 'Joseph's a loser... Joseph's a loser' was a bit of a clue.'

Joseph had indeed been having a bad day. News had travelled quickly throughout the village, and some people had not been particularly kind about the fact that his fiancée appeared to have... well... shall we say made a fool of him.

'Right,' said Mikey. 'Let's get this over and done with. I'll go down there... appear to Joseph in full angelic glory... and tell him that he's got to believe everything that Mary tells him. Okay?'

Gabe and Phin nodded in agreement.

'Right, here we go...'

Mikey dived gracefully over the side of the house.

Wish I could do that, thought Gabe. I bet he never crash-lands... I bet he never has a hair out of place... I bet he never...

'Argh!'

A scream suddenly erupted from the house below...

Followed by a crash...

And followed by Mikey - travelling at high speed - and coming to a screeching halt on the roof beside them. He looked somewhat flustered.

'Well?' asked Gabe.

'Not really,' confessed Mikey. 'I think he might have sort of fainted.'

Phin sighed.

'So much for the professional touch,' she muttered.

Two minutes later, all three angels were standing in Joseph's living room. Joseph himself was lying sprawled on the floor, snoring peacefully.

'What a mess,' sighed Phin.

'I'll say,' said Gabe.

He looked at the room around him. There were dirty dishes... unwashed washing... and half-finished woodwork projects scattered across every surface. It was a dump.

'I do hope Mary knows what she's letting herself in for,' he said.

'That's not for us to worry about,' said Phin. 'Now then...'

She gave Joseph an experimental nudge with

her foot. Joseph continued to snore contentedly.

'The first thing we need to do is get this young man up off the floor!'

'I was going to come back and pick him up,' muttered Mikey.

Phin ignored him.

'Everyone grab an arm and a leg,' she ordered. 'Now let's hoist him onto the bed!'

So, huffing and puffing, the three angels each grabbed Joseph's arms and legs and began to heave him towards the bedroom.

Suddenly…

'*Ow!*' yelled Mikey

He let go of Joseph and he began to hop about, grasping his foot.

'I trod on something!' he whimpered.

But the sudden movement threw Gabe and Phin off-balance, and they began to stagger under Joseph's weight.

'Look out!' said Phin.

'Why's he got his stupid tools scattered all over the floor?' moaned Mikey.

'I don't care,' snapped Phin. 'Just get back here and help us before - '

Bang!

Too late.

Joseph's head clonked against a bedside cabinet.

'Wurgh?' he said.

'He's waking up!' hissed Gabe.

'I can see that!' said Phin. 'Quick!

Mikey ran across to them and together, with one last mighty heave, they managed to dump Joseph – rather unceremoniously – onto the bed.

He began to stir.

'Everyone out of sight,' ordered Phin. 'Before he sees us and starts screaming the place down again.'

They all ran for cover. Mikey dived behind a sofa... Phin ran across the room and hid inside the wardrobe... Gabe looked around desperately...

'Under the bed,' hissed Phin.

Gratefully, Gabe dropped to the floor and rolled underneath - just as Joseph woke up fully. He sat up, rubbing his eyes.

'That was weird,' he said, 'I'm sure I saw... I mean, I thought I heard...'

He shook his head.

'No, that's ridiculous.'

Shaking his head, he swung his legs out of bed and disappeared off into the bathroom.

A few moments later, Gabe crawled out from under the bed.

'Urgh!' he gasped. 'He's got old socks under there and everything!'

He stood up and dusted himself down.

'He does appear to be somewhat allergic to the concept of laundry,' observed Phin, emerging from the wardrobe.

'So how are we going to deliver this message and get the wedding back on track?' said Mikey.

'Well we know your way didn't work,' muttered Phin.

'At least I tried,' Mikey snapped back.

'Okay, okay,' said Phin. 'There's no point in arguing about it now. Let's think carefully. We just need to come up with a plan.'

So they thought...

And then they thought some more…

And then…

They totally failed to come up with anything.

From the bathroom, they could hear the sounds of Joseph splashing about.

'What about a dream?' suggested Gabe.

Mikey and Phin exchanged confused glances.

'A dream?' said Phin.

'Yeah, it's simple,' said Gabe. 'All we do is wait until Joseph goes to sleep... and then we whisper in his ear that Mary was telling the truth... and that he needs to go ahead with the wedding… and then when he wakes up in the morning…'

'What?' said Mikey.

'Well, he'll think he's had some sort of vision… and… and he'll want to get married again…'

He trailed off. Mike and Phin looked at each other. Neither said anything. From the bathroom, the sound of taps stopped. Phin looked at Mikey.

'Have you got any better ideas?'

Mikey shook his head.

'Right then, let's give it a go.'

They quickly jumped back into their hiding places as they heard the sound of the bathroom door being unlocked. Joseph emerged. He was wearing pyjamas.

'Oh dear… oh dear… oh dear…' he muttered to himself as he got ready for bed… 'Why did Mary have to say all those things? We were all set for the wedding… It was going to be so lovely… And now suddenly she starts making up all these stories about angels… and babies! I mean; if she was worried about getting married, the least she could have done is come up with something *believable*. It's so ridiculous!'

He huffed and puffed and settled onto the bed.

Poor chap, thought Gabe from underneath, and I thought this message was supposed to make everyone happy…

A few minutes later, the sounds of breathing from above him became heavier. Cautiously, the three angels peered out.

'Clear!' whispered Mikey, giving the others a big thumbs up.

They emerged from their hiding places and tip-toed towards Joseph.

Suddenly...

'Teddy!' cried Joseph.

The three angels dived back into their hiding places, just as Joseph sat up in bed and opened his eyes.

'Can't go to sleep without you, Mr Snuggles, can we?' he said, getting up and retrieving a teddy bear from the far side of the room. He snuggled back into bed, clutching the slightly tatty bear and closed his eyes. His breathing became heavier again.

The angels peeped out. Once more, they began to creep towards Joseph.

'Hrtmngmhg!'

Joseph snorted.

Panicking, the angels dived back into their hiding places. Joseph sat up in bed and looked around the room.

'Huh,' he said.

He lay back down again, muttering to himself. The room became quiet once more. Cautiously, Gabe, Mikey and Phin crept out and began to approach the bed...

'Hiengnvwp!'

Joseph sat up. Quick as a flash, Phin flattened herself against the wall... Mikey flung himself to the floor... and Gabe...

Gabe panicked.

As Joseph rubbed his eyes, he looked around

in desperation – and then… *he spotted the teddy…*

On the spur of the moment, he picked it up and whacked Joseph over the head.

Thump!

Joseph collapsed onto the bed, instantly knocked out. He began to snore. The others stepped forwards. Phin stared in horror.

'What in Heaven's name do you think you're doing?!' she cried.

'He's asleep now,' said Gabe, sheepishly.

'He's *unconscious!* That's an entirely different matter!'

Mikey examined the recumbent Joseph.

'He's fine,' he said.

'That does *not* justify going around hitting people over the head with teddies!' fumed Phin.

'It got the job done,' said Gabe.

'True,' said Mikey.

'That is not the point. You could quite easily have done him an injury! What if he's got concussion?

What if he wakes up in the morning and has no idea who Mary is at all?'

'I didn't think of that,' confessed Gabe.

'Exactly!' squealed Phin, getting slightly hysterical. 'You know this man has a unique and special role to play in one of the most important moments in history. He has been chosen to help raise and look after God's own Son. It is completely inappropriate to go around hitting Biblical characters with cuddly toys!'

She stopped to catch her breath. Gabe sulked. Joseph snored.

'He's still unique and special,' muttered Gabe. 'He's just being it while he's asleep...'

'I am sorry but this is going to have to go in my official report when we get back home,' said Phin.

Mikey rolled his eyes.

'I saw that Michael!' she snapped.

'Look, can we just deliver the message and get out of here?' pleaded Mikey.

'Fine!' said Phin.

They turned back towards the bed where Joseph was.

Except that Joseph wasn't.

The bed was empty…

14

Clang!

The three angels stared at the bed in alarm.

'Where's he gone?' asked Mikey.

'I didn't hit him that hard,' said Gab.

'Right! Don't panic,' said Phin. 'Everyone look around. He can't have got that far.'

He hadn't. A quick search of the small house soon revealed Joseph to be in the kitchen... with a frying pan... attempting to cook bacon and eggs.

It was a peculiar sight.

Joseph was using biscuits for eggs... a banana for a sausage... and seemed to be attempting to cook them over a pair of shoes.

'Maybe I did hit him too hard,' wondered Gabe.

They all stared.

'It's weird,' said Mikey. 'His eyes are closed – and yet he looks like he's still asleep.'

'He can't be asleep; he's walking about,' said Gabe.

Phin shook her head.

'He's *sleepwalking*, you pair of numbskulls!' she said. A little too loudly.

At the sound of her voice, Joseph turned.

'*Mary?*' he asked. 'Is that you?'

Before Phin could say anything in reply, Joseph began lurching towards her, arms outstretched.

'Mary!' he cried.

Alarmed, Phin began to back away.

'Come here, my little Mary-wary,' crooned Joseph. 'Come and give your Jo-Jo a big kissy-wissy.'

Now Phin began to panic. Gabe stared open-mouthed… and Mikey sniggered… as she backed out of the room with the amorous Joseph lumbering after her.

'Somebody do something!' she squealed.

They followed as Phin dodged from room to room - around tables and over chairs - pursued by the sleep-walking Joseph (still holding the frying pan).

'I can't wait to tell everyone in Heaven about this,' giggled Mikey.

'We should do something' hissed Gabe.

They arrived back in the bedroom. There was nowhere else to go. Phin backed into a corner. Joseph moved towards her. There was no escape...

But there was the frying pan.

Snatching it from Joseph's hands, Phin swung it through the air and gave him a resounding whack around the head.

Clang!

Joseph collapsed onto the bed like a toppled tree. The three angels stared at one other in amazement.

'I wonder if I should mention this in my official report when I get back home?' smirked Mikey.

'Don't you dare,' muttered Phin.

Joseph snored.

'Now can we deliver the message?' asked Gabe.

'I'll do it,' said Phin.

She bent down next to the sleeping Joseph and whispered into his ear:

'Listen, Joseph,' she said. 'Here's the deal: Mary *did* see an angel. She *is* going to have a baby. He *is* going to be the Son of God. And you are *still* going to get married to her. Is that clear? Any questions?

Joseph snored.

'Good.'

She turned to the others.

'Now let's get out of here. And hope that this idea of yours has worked...'

The next morning, somewhat later than usual, Joseph woke up. He sat up in bed, scratching his head.

'What a weird dream,' he said to himself. 'All about angels... and then there was a bit about making breakfast... and...'

He paused.

He pulled something out from under the bed covers. It was the frying pan. Joseph's jaw dropped.

'It wasn't a dream!' he said. 'I really did make breakfast... and... and... I really did see an angel! So that means... that means... that means that Mary was telling the truth... and that means... that we can still get married!'

He leapt out of bed.

'Woohooo!'

15

Homeward Bound…?

Sounds of laughter and celebration filled the air.

Gabe and Phin were once again sitting on the roof of Mary's house, but this time they were listening to *happy* noises filtering up to them from the rooms down below. Mikey's head appeared above the edge.

'It's back on!' he grinned.

'Thank Heaven for that!' cried Phin, clapping her hands together.

Gabe breathed a sigh of relief. So their plan had worked… Mary and Joseph could now have a wonderful wedding… and everything would be set for the Son of God to be born.

'Mission accomplished,' grinned Mikey, hauling himself up onto the roof and sitting down next to them.

'Now we can see about getting ourselves back home.'

He ruffled Gabe's hair.

'Not bad for a first-timer.'

Gabe grinned.

'Well I must say it has been quite the adventure,' said Phin. 'Still, at least now we can say that The Event is - finally - officially well and truly underway!'

'Despite one or two complications,' said Gabe.

'None of which,' added Phin briskly, 'I feel need to be mentioned in the official record of events.'

'Agreed,' said Mikey.

Gabe grinned again. It felt good to have been part of something so big and important – and to not be getting into trouble for once. Maybe he was getting the hang of this angel lark after all?

'Right,' said Phin, standing up. 'Homeward bound!'

'You never know, there might be a bit of a fuss

when we get there,' she added, giving Gabe a wink.

And so, the three angels began to make preparations for the long journey home …

Completely unaware that they were being watched...

Deep in the shadows, in the corner of the courtyard, a pair of eyes appeared. They were not nice, friendly eyes. They glared up at the angels on the roof.

There was a cough and a wheeze, followed by a rasp and a voice spoke. It was not a nice, friendly voice.

'Well, well, well,' it said. 'Looks like we've got ourselves some angels here on planet earth... How very interesting.'

A second pair of eyes appeared, and a second voice spoke.

'What are they up to?'

This voice was smaller and more weasely, and seemed slightly worried that it was about to get into trouble with the first.

'I don't know yet,' hissed the first voice. 'But I think we ought to let the Boss know about this…'

16

A Snag

Heaven... the most wonderful place in the universe...

At last, they were home. Gabe, Mikey and Phin returned to the Great Citadel in triumph...

Where...

On the steps...

An enormous, cheering crowd had completely and utterly failed to materialise.

There were no banners...

No balloons...

Just a tall, thin angel standing there, holding a clipboard.

He cleared his throat.

'Er...' he said, hesitantly. 'There's been a snag.'

The snag was this:

The Emperor of Rome - a certain Caesar Augustus - had decided that a census should be taken of his entire empire.

'A what?' interrupted Gabe.

The three of them were sitting back in the courtyard near the Throne Room – the one with the statues and the little fountains. The nervous angel with the clipboard hovered nearby.

'It's like a sort of giant register,' said Phin.

Which was right - except that this was not a register for just one class at school – it was for every single person... everywhere.

(And it also had a lot of extra questions in it - like, how tall are you? And, what's your favourite colour? But that's not important here…)

The important thing was that the Roman Empire was huge, and happened to contain the country of Israel – where Mary and Joseph lived.

'Okay…' said Gabe, trying to understand. 'So they've got to answer a few questions. That doesn't sound too hard.'

'Indeed,' said the angel with the clipboard. 'However, there is the problem of *where* they are going to have to answer them...'

You see, just to make things fun - or awkward, depending on your point of view - the Roman Emperor had decided that, in order to take part in the census, each person had to return back to the town where they'd been born. Joseph came from a place called Bethlehem, and - since they were getting married - that meant that Mary was going to have to go to Bethlehem too.

Gabe leapt to his feet.

'Hang on a minute,' he cried. 'That's miles and miles away from where they live!'

The tall, thin angel checked his clipboard.

'Er... yes...' he acknowledged.

Gabe looked at the others.

'But Mary's about to have this baby. She can't go on a huge, long journey - not in her condition,' he protested.

'I believe that's why they're calling it a snag,' said Phin.

The tall, thin angel, shuffled his feet.

'I'd call it a complete and utter – ' began Mikey.

'Michael!' interrupted Phin. 'Now I'm sure this has all been thoroughly thought through. God must have known that this was going to happen. After all, he knows everything. I'm sure he's got it all in hand.'

'So what's going to happen?' said Gabe.

'Ah,' said the tall, thin angel, perking up. 'I'm glad you asked that. You see, you've been given new orders...'

17

After The Garden

Long ago...

There was a garden... and a tree...

(But you already know all this... unless you weren't paying attention... in which case I suggest you go back to the beginning of the book and start again – this time a bit more carefully.)

Anyway...

Adam and Eve ate the fruit from the tree... which was exactly what they'd been asked not to do... and, as a consequence, they were forced to leave the Garden of Eden forever.

They entered a world that was... well... like this one.

(In fact, it was this one.)

A world where if you fall over, you hurt your knee... a world where people sometimes get tummy aches or toothaches... A world where some people can be mean and grumpy... and not very nice.

A broken world.

Lucifer was delighted.

He'd managed to ruin God's plan...and mess up his friendships all at the same time.

God was heartbroken.

But he wasn't prepared to give up.

He was determined... he would bring his friends home... he would put the world back in order... he would put everything back the way it was meant to be once more...

He began to think of a plan...

18

Guard Duty

Time passed...

Gabe was very aware of time passing. You never really noticed it in Heaven, because of the general sort of 'now-ness' that I mentioned earlier. Plus everyone is so busy enjoying themselves that nobody cares what day of the week it is.

But here...

Down on planet earth...

Well, let's just say it was a little different...

The three angels had now been on the planet for more than eight months, and the novelty had *very* much worn off.

'Are we nearly there yet?' asked Gabe, as they trudged down the dusty desert road, following Mary, Joseph and their little donkey.

'Obviously not,' snapped Phin. 'And you asking the question every few miles is in no way helping us get there any quicker!'

They'd been on the road for weeks, accompanying Mary and Joseph as they made their way from their hometown to Bethlehem for the census.

'Stupid census,' muttered Gabe.

Orders had come through from Heaven's high command. As they were the so-called 'agents in the field'... and since they were already 'familiar with the situation' (that was how Mikey described it anyway), they had been given the task of escorting Mary and Joseph on their journey.

'It is an honour,' Phin had said.

But after miles and miles of travel, all Gabe knew was that he was hot... tired... and his wings were aching.

'Halt!' yelled Mikey.

They had arrived at a roadside inn, where Mary

and Joseph had chosen to rest for the night.

'Oh thank Heaven,' said Gabe, collapsing onto the ground.

Mikey strode over.

'Come on, soldier!' he barked enthusiastically. 'No time to rest. We need to establish a perimeter for the base camp.'

Grumbling, Gabe got to his feet again.

'For your information,' he said, 'I am not a soldier. I am a messenger.'

Mikey turned to him with a glint in his eye.

'And for your information,' he declared, 'the message has been delivered... and you are now under *my* command – which makes you a solider!'

He grinned. 'So look busy!'

Gabe groaned.

Outside the inn, Joseph gently helped Mary down from the donkey. She was extremely heavily pregnant now, and it wouldn't be long until the baby would be born. As they went inside, the sun began to set.

Slowly, Gabe trudged along as he patrolled the area around the inn. He paused and watched as Mikey concealed himself behind a wall... then dived out... and rolled...then sprinted and hid behind a tree.

'Clear!' he hissed to himself.

He's actually enjoying himself, thought Gabe. All these patrols... security arrangements... and hiding... and lying down in the muck and dirt...

I just wish he wouldn't make the rest of us take it so seriously.

He looked around.

Other than the road and the inn itself, the only things he could see for miles and miles were rocks... and hills... and the occasional small shrub...

Surely nothing bad was going to happen around here. Was it?

Gabe made his way back to the front of the inn. The cosy lights from the windows now cast long shadows onto the ground, as the sun finally slipped behind the hills and out of sight. Phin was by the front door, leaning against a wall.

'Won't be much longer now,' she said as he saw the gloomy look on Gabe's face.

'At least, I hope it won't be too much longer,' she added to herself. 'I must admit we are cutting it a little fine in getting Bethlehem in time for the baby to be born...'

Gabe said nothing.

'Still, cheer up! We'll be back in Heaven before you know it.'

'Unless they come up some other excuse for us to stay down here,' Gabe muttered.

'Now Gabe...'

'This whole thing's taking ages!' he blurted out. 'It was supposed to be a quick trip to deliver a message... nearly nine months ago! And now...

'Gabe...'

'I'm tired... I'm bored, and I want to go home.'

He sighed.

Phin waited for a moment, then said gently:

'I do understand. But, we have to be patient. There's nothing we can do that will get us to Bethlehem any quicker. Believe me, I wish there was. However… we are in the middle of something incredibly, wonderfully important here... something that is going to change the entire course of history. Don't you think that's exciting? Isn't that what you wanted?'

Gabe shrugged.

'I suppose,' he muttered.

'A front-row seat on history?'

'I never asked for a front-row seat,' said Gabe sulkily. 'I wanted a comfy seat with an armrest and a drinks holder – oh and one of those levers you can flip to make the front of the chair pop up.'

Phin smiled and patted him on the shoulder.

'It will all be worth it,' she reassured him.

'Believe me. And in the meantime, there's nothing you can do about it, so you may as well enjoy the journey. Now, I'd better go and check on Mary and Joseph.'

She gave him one last smile and then disappeared into the inn.

Gabe was left alone.

Apart from the donkey, which looked at him with a hopeful expression on its face. (Donkeys are always hopeful that they're going to get fed.)

Gabe scratched its ears, absent-mindedly. The donkey snorted. (There was no food, but a good scratch was second-best on the list of things it had been hoping for.)

And then Gabe had *the idea*.

There's no way we can get to Bethlehem any quicker, he thought to himself, unless...

He turned to look at the donkey. The donkey looked back at him, suspiciously.

Unless I can find a way to speed up the transport a little, thought Gabe.

'How do you fancy becoming the fastest donkey

ever in the history of the world?' he asked.

The donkey frowned. And backed away a little.

'It's okay' said Gabe. 'I'm a professional. I used to work in Heaven's Design Department with some of the best engineers in creation.' (He didn't mention that he'd been kicked out over that little incident with the two-headed chicken...)

'I just need to make a few adjustments. And besides,' he added. 'This isn't for me. This is to help Mary and Joseph; to help God's Great Plan for the universe come into being.'

He looked at the donkey, imploringly.

The donkey rolled its eyes.

Gabe took that as agreement.

'Yes!' he said, and began to roll up his sleeves...

19

L.C.

'What in Heaven's name do you think you are doing?' bellowed Phin.

It was a few minutes later. She had emerged from the inn and was now glaring across at Gabe.

Gabe froze.

He had a large wrench in one hand... and the other was elbow-deep in the donkey's side...

'Er...' he said.

A leg fell off the donkey. The donkey didn't seem bothered. It just rolled its eyes and carried on munching a carrot.)

'I was trying to make the donkey go a bit faster...' said Gabe sheepishly. 'You know, to help Mary and Joseph get to Bethlehem a bit quicker? You said there was nothing we could do, and I thought...'

He trailed off. Phin did not look impressed.

'You *know* that sort of thing is strictly forbidden!' she scolded.

'But I thought... you know... in the circumstances...'

'*Forbidden!*'

Gabe looked at the floor.

'Now put everything back where you found it, at once. *Exactly* where you found it! Honestly, Gabe, sometimes I really do wonder if you're ever going to become a proper angel.'

She turned on her heel and strode back into the inn.

Gabe sighed.

He looked at the donkey. The donkey looked back and seemed to sort of shrug its shoulders. (I know donkeys can't – but you get the idea.)

Slowly, Gabe started to pick up all the spare parts and began putting the donkey back in its proper order.

Why does everything have to be so difficult? he thought. All he was supposed to do was deliver a message... But then that had gone wrong and then he'd had to fix a wedding... And then there was this business with the census... I mean, surely God *knew* it was going to happen? Surely it would have been easier for the baby to have been born beforehand – or even afterwards? Why did it have to be right in the middle? It didn't make any sense. It was almost as if everything was being made difficult on purpose...

This might well be God's Great Plan from since before the beginning of time, grumbled Gabe, but to my mind, it all seems a bit of a mess.

He sighed again and carried on repairing the donkey.

A figure appeared.

'Appeared' is probably the right word to use. One moment, there was nothing there – the next, there was.

The night was full of shadows and from one of them, at the side of the road, the figure had emerged.

It looked like a man... but... slightly wrong.

Slightly too tall... slightly too angular...

It was as though someone who is right-handed had done their best drawing of a person – but with their *left* hand. It just wasn't quite correct – although it was difficult to say exactly what was wrong.

The figure was dressed in an effort to impress. It wore a top hat... a tailcoat... and a cane with a silver decoration at the top. It was entirely the wrong sort of fashion; the sort of thing that was probably really fashionable, but in a different time zone and a completely different country.

It spoke.

'Good evening,' it said.

The voice was... well, wonderful to be honest. It seemed to speak of promises... and delights... and desires... and dreams fulfilled.

Gabe jumped, startled.

'What? Where did you come from?'

'Oh, I just happened to be in the neighbourhood,' said the figure.

Its face was still in shadow, but Gabe was sure it had a smile on its face.

'I must say, I am intrigued,' said the figure, starting to advance towards where Gabe was standing. 'Fancy discovering a group of angels, just hanging about here on the Earth.'

'Who are you?' demanded Gabe.

'Oh, I do apologise,' chuckled the figure. 'Allow me to introduce myself. My name is... well, my friends call me L.C.'

'L.C...'

'It's a sort of nickname.'

Gabe gasped.

'Hang on a minute,' he cried. 'I know who you are! You're... you're...'

L.C. interrupted 'Lucifer? The bad guy? The enemy? The great deceiver? The angel of light? The morning star? I do seem to go by a lot of different names these days.'

'But... but...'

Gabe began backing away...

'Oh, please don't be alarmed.'

'But you're evil.'

L.C. chuckled.

'I much prefer the term 'misunderstood,' he said.

Gabe looked around, frantically. Where were Mikey and Phin when he needed them?

'You know, I'm really not that bad,' said L.C., flashing a charming smile. 'I bet if you were to hear my side of the story... You see, those folks in Heaven tend to only give out one version of events these days... I think if you were to listen to mine... you might find it... intriguing.'

He took a step closer.

'You know,' he continued, 'I used to be just like you – full of enthusiasm, wanting to make a difference... I worked hard... I did as I was told... went the extra mile... I honestly tried my very best... But somehow it was never quite good enough...'

Gabe said nothing.

'No one recognised my talents... no one appreciated my ideas... no one understood.'

L.C. looked sad for a moment.

'They just didn't get me,' he whispered, looking off into the distance, his voice choking with emotion.

Gabe stayed silent. He wasn't sure what to think anymore.

'And, then one day...' said L.C, spinning back to face Gabe.

'They turned against me - threw me out! All because I asked for a bit of recognition for once.'

He paused dramatically.

'But,' he added...

His smile suddenly snapping back...

'It turned out to be the best thing that ever happened! Now I am free to be myself! I can go where I want; do what I want... No one leaning over my shoulder... No one saying 'do this'... 'don't do that'... I'm my own boss... And the only person I need to please is... well, me!'

He laughed. The laughter was... infectious, almost enchanting.

'Sounds... good...' said Gabe.

'Oh, it is - believe me!' L.C. beamed. 'Now I can do whatever I want – whenever I want! If I feel like getting up at half-past two in the afternoon – I can do that. If I want to eat cream cakes and strawberry jam all day – I can do that too!'

He laughed again.

'And so could *you*. After all,' he added, 'it's got to be better than being a...what are you...a babysitter?'

'Hang on a minute; I'm not *just* a babysitter,' said Gabe.

L.C. raised his eyebrows.

'Oh, really?'

'Yeah. You see this is a really important baby,' said Gabe.

'He's part of God's Great Plan to change the whole of the world... and free the human race from... from...'

He faltered.

'The likes of me?' suggested L.C.

'I probably shouldn't have said that, should I?' said Gabe, his cheeks beginning to turn red.

'But I'm so glad you did,' grinned L.C.

'I... I... I'd better go. I probably shouldn't be talking to you.'

Gabe started backing away.

'Remember what I told you!' L.C. called after him.

'Er, well… yes indeed… anyway got to go… lots to do…'

Gabe stumbled off towards the inn.

L.C. watched him go. From the shadows behind him, appeared two pairs of eyes. (The same unfriendly ones that we'd seen before.)

'Trouble, Boss?' asked a voice.

'Hmmm, perhaps…' pondered L.C. 'It would seem that God is planning to try and put an end to my little empire down here. Well, that can't be allowed to happen. I must stop these meddling angels and their confounded scheme if it's the last thing I do… And if I don't… it might be!'

20

The Battle

Long ago...

Before the beginning of everything...

(Even before the tree...)

There was Heaven... there was God... there were the angels...

And there was L.C...

(Or Lucifer, as he was known back then). The best, the brightest, the cleverest angel of them all.

The problem was that he knew it...

He knew that he was good... and he knew that he was special... And he began to get ideas... Ideas about not just being a servant anymore...Ideas about being The Boss... He began to plot...

With cunning words and tricksy ways, he persuaded a number of other angels to join him...

And together they tried to take God's throne...

A terrible battle took place...

For many days and nights, the armies of Heaven - led by the archangel Mikey - fought against L.C. and his rebellious crew...

Until finally...

God's army prevailed.

The rebels were thrown out of Heaven... and they tumbled down onto the world below...

There L.C. wandered, planning his revenge...

Until, one day...

He happened to spot a certain tree...

21

Worries

The road ran onwards...

Mile by mile... and step by step... Gabe, Mikey and Phin - and, of course, Mary and Joseph - inched their way gradually closer to Bethlehem. Past village after village... town after town... (And the occasional group of waiting bandits - who were always extremely surprised to be greeted by a grinning Mikey, brandishing his sword.)

'Halt!'

Mikey's voice rang out across the landscape. Mary and Joseph had stopped for a rest at a shady spot by the roadside.

'*Perimeter!*' yelled Mikey.

Gabe and Phin knew the drill well enough by now, and quickly got themselves into their usual guard positions.

Gabe was flapping.

(Not 'flapping' as in waving his wings and flying about – more 'flapping' as in being bothered and anxious and in a bit of a muddle.)

What am I to do? he thought. I've only gone and given away the secrets of God's Great Plan – and to God's archenemy at that!

Of course, he knew what he *should* do - he should tell the others. The trouble is, that was the one thing that he really, really *didn't* want to do.

He was embarrassed, for starters.

And worried.

After all, what would they say?

Actually, he knew what they'd probably say. They'd go ballistic... they'd shout at him... tell him off... and then...

And then they'd send him back to Heaven.

In disgrace... a failure...

'Typical Gabe,' everyone would say, 'made a mess of everything again.'

He couldn't face that. But what *was* he to do?

He watched as Mikey crept along behind a tree nearby... then dived out... rolled... and ran behind another.

'Clear!' Mikey hissed.

Or maybe, thought Gabe to himself, maybe everything will be okay. After all, we've got Mikey with us – the captain of the angelic guard. There's not much that can go wrong when he's around. He'll make sure they were safe enough - after all, that's why he's here with us.

Besides, the others probably already knew that L.C. was lurking about - and hadn't told him. Yes, that was probably it. He was always the last person to know about anything important anyway. And hadn't there been hints about that sort of thing? That must be the reason why Mikey was insisting on all these security routines.

Yes, that was it. No point in saying anything. The other two would probably laugh at him for even reporting it.

'Silly old Gabe,' they'd say, 'always worrying about everything.'

He began to feel a bit better.

But, as Gabe gazed around at the surrounding countryside, his eyes suddenly fell on a dense patch of trees nearby. It was filled with shadows.

He stared.

Was it his imagination or did some of the shadows seem darker than others?

'*Hello*,' said a voice.

Gabe almost leapt out of his skin.

He spun around...

And saw Mary standing, a few metres away.

'Sorry,' she said. 'I didn't mean to give you a scare.'

'Oh no, no, you didn't,' Gabe muttered quickly. 'Not at all. I was just guarding in the... erm... other direction...'

Mary smiled.

'Well I'm sorry for interrupting you,' she said. I was just hoping to sit down in the shade under this tree? If you don't mind. I could do with getting out of the sun.'

'Of course,' said Gabe.

He stepped out of the way. Mary carefully settled herself onto the ground next to the tree. She looked up at him.

'Don't you ever need a rest?' she asked.

'Me? Oh no!' he answered smartly. 'We angels never get tired.'

(And we're also never supposed to be able to tell lies, he added to himself – although he didn't say that bit out loud. Why *did* he say that? Must be all the time on earth getting to him...)

'Won't be long now,' said Mary.

'About another five or six miles, I think.'

'No,' she said, smiling. 'I meant it won't be long until the baby arrives.'

'Oh... er... yes...'

Gabe had been so preoccupied with the challenges of the journey recently that he hadn't given much thought to the actual arrival of the baby.

'Er, yes, I guess it's not too long now.'

'I can't wait to meet him,' said Mary. 'I wonder what he'll be like... It's hard to imagine, isn't it? God himself... here on earth... in human form... '

She placed a hand on her bump.

'It seems incredible, doesn't it? He's going to change the world. He's going to bring hope and meaning to billions...'

She closed her eyes, lost in the wonder of it all. Gabe shuffled his feet.

'Well... er... I suppose I better...'

Mary opened her eyes.

'I won't keep you,' she said. 'I know you've got a very important job to do; getting us to Bethlehem safely. And on time,' she added laughing.

Gabe saluted awkwardly. Then wandered off to take up another guard position, a short distance away...

'How very exciting!'

This was a different voice. Gabe spun around again.

Where had it come from? There was no one else about. Then his eyes fell on a shadowy patch in the trees nearby - and he realised that one of the shadows was staring back. An evil-looking pair of eyes gleamed out at him. A grin appeared beneath them.

'What an extraordinary-sounding baby!' said the same voice, which belonged to the evil-looking eyes.

A second pair of eyes appeared.

'We can't wait to meet him,' added the second voice.

Both voices sniggered.

'Go away,' hissed Gabe.

'Oh dear! You're going to have to start being nicer to us,' said the first voice.

'Especially as you'll want to join us after you get kicked out of Heaven,' laughed the second. 'After all, they're hardly going to want you there when they found out you've messed up God's Big Plan with the baby!'

'Look, I'm warning you,' said Gabe.

'Oooh, no!' cried the first voice, sarcastically. 'The little angel's warning us – how very scary! Boo hoo hoo!'

They both pretended to cry.

'Right, that's it,' said Gabe.

He picked up a stick and threw it into the shadows. The voices just laughed even harder.

And then Mikey charged...

'Yeeearrgggh!'

With a blood-curdling war cry, he came hurtling across the grass towards them, his mighty sword drawn, a fearsome look on his face. The eyes in the shadows grew as round as saucers. Whimpering, they vanished from sight.

Mikey staggered to a halt next to Gabe. He sheaved his sword, a look of satisfaction on his face.

'You okay?' he asked.

Gabe nodded.

'Pesky creatures,' said Mikey, looking towards the shadows. 'Always lurking around somewhere. Those ones aren't too bad, although they can give you a bit of a scare if you're not ready for them. Don't you worry, though. They won't be back in a hurry.'

'Although,' he added, still staring into the shadows, 'if *those* ones know that we're here... then their boss might too... and that could be a problem.'

'Still,' he said, turning back to Gabe 'as long as they don't know *exactly* what we're up to, we should be fine. Come on; the sooner get to Bethlehem the better!'

Gabe said nothing.

22

Bethlehem

'Now that is a sight for sore eyes!' said Mikey.

It was the next day and the three angels were standing at the top of a hill. Before them, about a mile ahead, lay the town of Bethlehem – its lights twinkling in the early evening dusk.

Gabe felt himself begin to relax. Perhaps they were going to make it after all...

'Well done, everyone,' said Phin. 'One last little push and then it's celebration time.'

'Celebration time?' asked Gabe.

'Oh, yes,' said Phin. 'The birth of this child is going to be quite the occasion! The Heavenly choirs have been practicing for years... and there is something rather special being planned with the stars – although that's all rather hush-hush at the moment.'

Just at that moment, Mary winced. Joseph rushed over and began to fuss around her.

'I'm fine, I'm fine,' she kept saying.

'Still,' added Phin. 'No point in dilly-dallying. That baby's not going to wait forever. Come on; let's get ourselves down the road and find those two a nice place to stay.'

Bethlehem was busy...

I don't mean just a little bit busy - I mean hugely, *massively*, *enormously* busy.

You could hardly move for all the people. They were on the roads... they were on the pavements... they stood in doorways... they hung out of windows... they sat on roofs... they sat on each other...

(By that, I mean that the children were sitting on their parent's shoulders - anything else would be unkind.)

There were people of all different ages... with all different accents… from all across the country of

Israel. Some of them seemed excited. Some of them just looked tired. But all of them had one thing in common: they were all looking for somewhere to stay.

As night fell, Mary and Joseph joined the throng, heading down the main road towards the centre of town...

'It's a bit busy,' said Gabe.

The three angels had positioned themselves on the rooftop of a large hotel (much to the surprise of a local family of pigeons). Gabe peered over the edge watching as, down below, Mary and Joseph wove their way through the crowded streets of the town.

'Don't worry,' said Phin, who was sitting, leaning against a chimney. 'The hardest part was getting here. All they need to do now is find a nice hotel or an inn or something.'

'Well I hope they find somewhere soon,' said Gabe.

'Patience,' said Phin. 'Everything is going to

be fine now.'

She leaned back and closed her eyes.

'You'll see.'

But, two hours later...

'It's a bit busy,' said Phin who was now peering over the edge. Behind her, Mikey and Gabe were pacing up and down on the rooftop - although this was now a different rooftop...

They had followed Mary and Joseph as their search had led them from the centre of Bethlehem (with its nice hotels and inns), all the way to the outskirts of the town which were... well... less nice.

The hotels had gone from being five-star to... well, one-star.

(And some didn't even have that.)

And still, they hadn't found anywhere to stay.

'There must be somewhere,' muttered Phin.

'There'd better be,' said Gabe. 'Otherwise, that baby's going to be born out on the streets.'

'Not on my watch,' growled Mikey.

'Now, let's not panic yet,' said Phin, (who actually looked as though she was about to start panicking.) 'I'm sure that not *every* inn or hotel in Bethlehem can be full.'

She forced a chuckle. The others looked at her.

'Can they?' she said.

Down below, in the backstreets of Bethlehem, an exhausted Mary slipped down from the donkey's back and settled herself at the side of the road to rest.

'There, there,' said Joseph, as he fussed around - patting her hand, rubbing her back and generally trying to act in an encouraging way.

(Although, to be honest, it looked as though Joseph was the one who needed the encouragement.)

'There.. there... there...' he kept repeating.

Mary smiled. And then winced.... and then tried to smile... and then winced again as she felt the baby's imminent arrival.

'Won't be long now,' she gasped.

Joseph whimpered.

'There, there,' he said again.

(As much to himself as to anyone else.)

Mary took his hand.

'Don't worry,' she said. 'Everything's going to be okay. We'll find somewhere to stay. Something's bound to turn up soon. God won't let us down. He is with us.'

Joseph didn't look convinced. Mary gently took his hand and placed it on her bump.

'He's *with* us,' she repeated, looking him earnestly in the eyes.

'He won't let us down.'

'I know,' said Joseph. 'I know. I understand all that, but… we've been searching for hours and hours, and… '

He paused as Mary winced again.

'We're running out of time…'

'What are we going to do?' asked Gabe.

He, Mikey and Phin were huddled together on the rooftop above.

'I don't know,' bumbled Phin. 'I don't know. Nobody ever mentioned anything about needing to book a room. Our job was simply to get them here.'

'Well we have to do *something*,' said Gabe. 'That baby's going to be here any minute - with or without a place to stay.'

'But what *can* we do?' said Phin. 'We can hardly just build a new hotel… or kick someone else out of their room...'

'We could,' grunted Mikey.

'But we're not going to,' Phin snapped back.

'My job is to keep them safe and well,' said Mikey. 'And that does not involve having the Son of God being born out on the streets!'

'Okay, okay!' said Gabe, holding his hands and stepping between them before anyone could lose their temper.

'Let's think,' he continued. 'There *must* be somewhere. Maybe we're supposed to help them look for it?'

They thought about this for a second.

'But we can't exactly go around knocking on doors,' said Phin. 'People will start panicking if they see a load of angels.'

'That's true…' said Gabe.

'But,' he added - eyeing some clothes on a washing line nearby - 'I think I've got an idea...'

23

Knock, knock

'I feel stupid,' said Mikey.

It was a short while later, and the three angels stood facing each in a back alley.

It has to be said, they did look a little ridiculous.

By raiding all the washing lines in the area, they had managed to acquire an interesting selection of coats, shirts, trousers, hats etc. and were now wearing them - although not in a particularly coordinated or fashionable order.

They looked... well, they looked rather odd. But at least they looked a lot less like three angels - and now rather more like three passable human beings (if rather oddly dressed ones).

'We're going to get into so much trouble for this when we get back home,' muttered Phin.

'We'll worry about that later,' said Gabe.

'So what now?' asked Mikey, who was feeling uncomfortable (and not only with the clothing...)

'We split up and find somewhere for Mary and Joseph to stay,' said Gabe. 'Meet back here in half an hour?'

The others nodded.

'Let's do it,' said Mikey.

A few minutes later, Gabe was weaving his way through the teeming throng in the streets of Bethlehem. He spotted an inn and approached the front door.

Knock! Knock!

'Yes?' came a quavering voice from within.

The door half opened and a little old lady peered out through the crack.

'Oh, excuse me,' said Gabe, bending down slightly.

(She was *very* small.)

'I was wondering if you could help me? I'm

looking for a room for the night.'

'Eh?'

'A room for the night,' he repeated, slightly louder.

'A room for a kite?' asked the little old lady, who was clearly not only very small and very old, but also rather hard of hearing.

Gabe was confused.

'Er, no - not *kite*,' he said. 'Night!'

'Eh?'

'Night! Night!'

He was almost shouting now.

'Oh,' said the little old lady, with a smile. 'Night, night to you too!'

She gave him a cheerful wave and began to close the door.

'No, wait!' said Gabe desperately.

She paused.

He took a deep breath.

'I... need... a... *rooooom*...' he said, enunciating

each word as clearly and carefully as he possibly could.

'Oh!'

Her face lit up.

'Why didn't you say so? Just a minute!'

She ducked inside.

Gabe breathed a sigh of relief. He began to feel hopeful.

Until she returned - holding a broom.

(You know, the sort of thing you use for brushing the floor? Or maybe you don't. Anyway...)

Gabe stared.

'Not *broom*,' he said, through gritted teeth. '*Room! Room! Somewhere to stay!*'

'Oh, I see' she said, realisation at last dawning on her face.

'Sorry - we're full.'

She closed the door.

Gabe plodded on. Perhaps this wasn't going to be as straightforward as he'd thought. As he headed off in search of the next inn, a drop of rain fell from the sky...

Knock! Knock!

He rapped at the door of another dingy-looking inn, a little further down the road.

'No!' yelled an angry voice.

Gabe looked around. And then looked up - and saw that the angry voice belonged to an angry face peering down at him from an upstairs window.

'I haven't asked anything yet,' he said.

'Well, what do you want?' snapped the angry face.

'A room for the night?' asked Gabe, hopefully.

'No chance - we're full! And the way things are going, we're going to be full for the rest of the year! So clear off!'

The angry face disappeared inside, and the window slammed shut. With a sigh, Gabe turned and headed on down the road.

Knock, knock!

Another street, another door…

This one belonged to a tiny bed and breakfast, tucked around a corner just off the main road. A hatch in the door slid back. A tired-looking face appeared.

'Yes?' asked a tired-sounding voice, which belonged to the tired-looking face.

'I don't suppose you have any rooms?' asked Gabe (although not in a particularly hopeful way, as this was now the umpteenth time he'd asked the same question that night).

'Er, yes,' said the voice. 'Of course we do.'

Gabe's heart leapt.

'But I'm afraid they're all full,' added the voice. 'Try again next year!'

Gabe's heart sank. He turned and trudged off once more into the night.

It began to rain properly…

Everywhere Gabe went, it was the same story - grumpy faces... tired voices... slammed doors... and no room. Anywhere. Not a bed... not a sofa... not even a comfy chair. It seemed that every single inn... every guesthouse... every hotel in Bethlehem was full that night.

Gabe was now desperate.

Surely this wasn't how things were meant to go? This was 'The Event' - God's Great Big Plan from beyond the dawn of time - surely His Son couldn't be born out on the streets?

'Well?' he asked, a short while later.

He, Mikey and Phin were huddled back on a rooftop. Nobody said anything in response, but he could tell from their faces that none of them had managed to find anywhere to stay.

That was it... they tried... and they'd failed. And now the greatest moment in history was about to be... well... a bit of a disaster, to be honest.

The rain – which had previously been a light drizzle – chose that moment to become a full-blown downpour.

Down in the street below, Mary sheltered in a doorway, trying to keep out of the now torrential rain. The donkey nuzzled into her, doing his best to protect her from the worst of the weather.

From the other end of the street, Joseph ran towards them, splashing his way through the puddles.

'There's a stable,' he gasped, as he arrived next to her, panting and slightly out of breath.

'A stable?' said Mary.

'Round the back of one of the inns. The innkeeper said he didn't mind us using it.'

'As long as it's dry, I'll go anywhere,' said Mary.

And with that, Joseph helped her to her feet and they headed off down the street…

'*A stable?*' said Mikey.

Phin opened her mouth... then closed it ... then opened it again.

'I suppose it's better than nothing,' she said at last, sounding extremely uncertain about it.

Mikey shook his head.

'How are we going to tell everyone?' asked Gabe.

'Don't worry, they'll know for themselves soon enough,' snorted Mikey. 'In a minute, half of Heaven'll be turning up for the celebrations.'

'Celebrations?' said Gabe.

'This is still one of the most important moments in history,' said Phin.

'One of the most embarrassing ones,' muttered Mikey.

'Admittedly things haven't gone entirely to plan,' Phin snapped back. 'However, this is still the start of God's Great Plan... and we should... we should make the best of it!'

The rain poured.

'Right, then,' said Mikey. 'I'd better get on guard duty.'

He disappeared off into the evening's gloom.

Phin turned to Gabe.

'And, I erm...' she said. 'I'd better go and liaise with the celebration committee...'

She gave him a weak smile. Then she too headed off into the night. Gabe was left alone.

Or was he...?

Nearby, a pair of eyes gleamed out of the darkness. For a moment there was just the hint of a smile... and then the darkness fell again.

24

An Offer

A short while later, Gabe trudged his way through the dirty streets of Bethlehem, which were now running with muddy water.

A stable? he thought to himself.

All those years of preparations... choirs of angels ready to burst into song... and the Son of God is going to be born in a dirty, muddy, smelly stable... What a mess!

Come to think of it, the whole thing's been a disaster from start to finish:

Joseph not believing Mary...

The wedding nearly getting cancelled...

The census...

That long, difficult journey...

And now...

Now there's not even a proper place for the baby to be born!

What was that about?

How hard would it have been to have some-how… some way… made a room available? (Or at the very least to have prompted Joseph to book ahead…)

The whole thing was a shambles.

And yet...

This was supposed to be God's Great Plan for his creation – something that he'd been preparing since the dawn of time.

Gabe couldn't understand it. None of it made sense. It seemed such a mess.

He kicked a stone into an alley.

To his surprise, it was kicked back out again. He paused and peered into the entranceway.

'Hi,' said a voice.

Gabe jumped, startled. Leaning against a wall was the tall, dark figure of L.C.

'How's it going?' he asked.

He stepped out of the alleyway and strolled over towards Gabe.

'Still doing the whole secret mission thing?'

'Oops!' he cried, putting a finger to his lips and pretending to be embarrassed as Gabe looked around in alarm.

'Well?' asked L.C.

'Not very well,' admitted Gabe.

'That's a shame,' said L.C. 'After all that hard work... all that effort... all those months of waiting around - not being allowed to use any shortcuts... all that traipsing through the desert...'

He tutted and shook his head sadly.

'Still, I'm sure they'll all be very grateful to you up there in Heaven. I'm sure when you get back they'll all be lining the streets… cheering your name... waiting to shake your hand…'

He broke off, laughing. (It wasn't a very nice laugh.)

'Or perhaps not!' he added.

Gabe looked glum.

'Oh but, don't worry,' said L.C. 'You won't be forgotten. How could you be? After all, you're the angel Gabriel – the angel who was in charge of the greatest fiasco in history! You're going to be famous!'

Gabe scowled and began to walk away.

'Oh but please, don't take this badly. Excuse my fun. You and I both know none of this is your fault. *You're* not to blame. No matter what anyone else says.

The whole thing was a mess from the start. No one explained to you what was really going on - even though the big guy is supposed to be 'all-knowing' and 'all-wise.' (Of course, he could be getting a bit forgetful in his old age - he has been knocking around for a while.)'

Gabe sat down.

'I'll be honest with you,' said L.C., coming to sit next to him. 'You're not the first person to be messed around. I remember it so well. It all starts out so exciting... you've been chosen for a special task...

it's going to be world-changing. They send you off full of enthusiasm... and then one after another all these obstacles suddenly start to appear. And not a sign, not a hint of any help from above. Sound familiar?'

Gabe nodded.

L.C. shook his head sadly.

'Sometimes I wonder if they're just incompetent up there or simply cruel. I really do. And we're supposed to be the bad guys...'

Behind him, in the shadows, other eyes appeared. They were trying their best to appear friendly.

'Just because we don't want to play by Heaven's rules anymore,' continued L.C. 'And why should we? We want to be free. We want to have a little fun. Is that so bad?'

Gabe shook his head.

'You know,' said L.C. turning to him, 'you could always join us. We're a jolly little bunch – footloose and fancy-free. Just doing what we want when we want. No one telling us what to do. No one telling us where to go. No rules... no 'do's... no 'don't s....'

He smiled at Gabe.

'Sounds pretty good, eh?'

Gabe nodded. Right at that moment, sitting there in the rain, it did indeed sound pretty good.

'There's just one thing I'd need from you,' said L.C.

'What's that?' asked Gabe.

'The baby; hand it over to me. Call it a sign of commitment, if you like.

Gabe gasped.

'After all, I am offering you freedom, acceptance and everything you have ever wanted. There's just a little price to pay.'

He stood up

'Give it some thought,' he said.

With that, he flashed a final grin and wandered off into the night...

25

The Stable

The rain was getting heavier. (If that was possible.) It was now bouncing off the streets and running in streams down the gutters. Thunder could be heard rumbling in the distance. Gabe arrived at the stable. He shook off his wings, opened the door and crept inside.

It was an extraordinary sight.

The baby had been born and was now wrapped in an old shawl and lying in a manger at the centre of the dingy room. Next to him sat Mary, singing a gentle lullaby. (Joseph was snoozing in a corner).

Outside, the wind raged and the rain pounded, and yet this tiny wooden room was filled with the most wonderful sense of peace that Gabe had ever known.

From the corners of the stable, the donkey, two cows, a couple of sheep and a stray hen watched fascinated - whilst keeping a respectful distance.

Gabe gently knocked on a wooden beam.

Mary looked up.

'Oh it's you,' she said. '*You* don't need to knock.'

'Oh… I just thought that... I mean.. erm... I didn't want to interrupt,' he stammered.

Mary smiled.

'It's okay,' she said.

'I'm really sorry about all this,' he said, indicating the stable and the general mess around (and the bucket that had been placed to catch some drips from the roof). 'I never imagined that things would end up, well… like *this*.'

'I don't mind,' said Mary.

'What, being stuck in a smelly, old stable? No offence,' he added for the benefit of some of the animals who were looking a little put out.

'Honestly, it's fine,' said Mary. 'Yes, it's not exactly how *I* imagined things would be, but... I'm sure it's exactly how *God* imagined it would be. And I *trust* him. He knows what he's doing, after all.'

Gabe said nothing.

Mary picked up the sleeping baby and cradled him gently in her arms.

'Would you like to see him?' she asked.

Gabe nodded. Very carefully, he stepped forwards. (Careful partly because he didn't want to disturb the baby, and partly because you never know what you're going to find on the floor in a stable.)

He stared at the tiny, fragile newborn child, who was just beginning to wake up.

'Is that... Him? he asked.

'Jesus,' said Mary. 'God's own Son.'

Gabe stared, transfixed.

'Would you like to hold him?'

'Me?'

'Why not?'

'Er... oh... okay..' Gabe stammered.

With great care, Mary placed the precious bundle in his arms.

'He's beautiful,' he breathed.

And he truly was. He was the most beautiful thing that Gabe had ever seen.

'Actually, I wonder if you could do me a favour,' said Mary. 'I'm feeling ever-so tired. Would you mind holding him for a little bit whilst I go and have a lie-down?'

Gabe looked startled, then nodded.

'Er… yes.. of course.'

'Thank you.'

Mary wandered off to the far side of the barn, leaving Gabe alone. (Apart from the animals who weren't particularly paying him attention anymore – not since they'd worked out that he wasn't going to feed them.)

Gabe stared down at Jesus, lying in his arms. Here was God himself – the great Creator of the universe – made into the form of a tiny little baby.

'Hello,' said Gabe.

Jesus looked back at him. He gurgled happily, his eyes shining.

Gabe felt his heart melting.

He's smiling at me, thought Gabe. He knows all my faults, all my rubbish thoughts… and yet he's still smiling at me. He's the Lord of the whole universe – and he likes *me*... Oh, what am I going to do?

26

The Chase

A short while later, a loose panel in the wall of the stable swung open, and Gabe slipped through into the street outside. In his arms, he held a tightly wrapped bundle.

Thunder rumbled ominously and lightning flashed across the sky. A particularly bright flash illuminated the figure of L.C., sheltering beneath the eaves of a house.

'Well?' he demanded. 'Is that him?'

Gabe said nothing.

'Hand him over to me.'

Thunder crashed overhead. Rain pounded on the roofs.

But Gabe didn't move.

'Look, we haven't got all night, ' said L.C., a

hint of menace creeping into his voice.

'Now hand… it… over!'

'I'm not sure,' said Gabe.

'Think about what I am offering you: a chance to escape from the drudgery of Heaven, with all its rules and regulations. I am offering you a life of luxury and freedom and everything your heart desires. All you have to do is give... me... the... baby!'

'The thing is,' said Gabe, 'I quite like him.'

'What?!'

L.C. stepped forward.

'Listen to me, you stupid angel,' he hissed, (now completely abandoning any pretence of niceness). 'I am the only chance that you've got. Remember how God abandoned you on the journey? Remember how angry he's going to be with you when he finds out how you've messed everything up?'

From the shadows behind LC, a pair of eyes appeared. Followed by another... and another...

And another...

And suddenly it seemed as though every shadow, every corner of the narrow street was filled with gleaming, watching eyes. None of them seemed friendly.

Gabe looked down at the bundle in his arms.

'You know, I'm not so sure,' he said.

He looked up at L.C.

'You see, I don't think God is going to be angry. And I don't think he did abandon us on the journey. I think he was here with us all along.'

'*Give me the baby!*'

'No.'

L.C. snarled.

'There's nothing you can offer me,' said Gabe, 'no treasure, no reward - that's ever going to be greater than this. You see, all I ever wanted was to feel special... and accepted... and valued for who I am... And, guess what? I just discovered I already am.'

'Well said, Gabe,' shouted Mikey, as he and Phin appeared from round the corner.

L.C. glanced around at them, anxiously. He turned back to Gabe.

'Last chance,' he said.

Gabe shook his head.

'Well, in that case…'

Suddenly, L.C. lunged forwards and reached out for the bundle in Gabe's arms. Gabe stepped backwards, slipping on the mud and staggering against the stable wall...

At the same moment, L.C.'s creatures from the shadows leapt forwards and swarmed toward Mikey and Phin…

Phin shrieked. Mikey drew his sword and ran forwards to meet them, yelling a battle cry...

L.C. loomed over Gabe. He bent down and took the bundle from his arms.

'That'll do nicely,' he said - and leapt off into the night.

Gabe scrambled to his feet and looked towards the rooftops, where the figure of L.C. could be made out, scampering away. He set off after him.

Thunder rumbled overhead...

Further down the alley, Mikey had made short work of the first of the creatures that had come towards him. (The cleverer ones had run off as soon as they'd seen his sword.)

Phin was having a little more trouble. One of the shadow creatures was sitting on her head with its hands over her eyes, and she was running round and round in circles, shrieking 'I can't see! I can't see!' With a grunt, Mikey reached out and plucked the creature from her, then launched it with a drop kick into a stack of bins at the far end of the street.

'Thank you,' said Phin.

Meanwhile, up on rooftops, Gabe skidded and slid in the rain. He could see L.C. a few buildings further on from him, leaping nimbly from roof-top to roof-top.

L.C. glanced over his shoulder and stared in surprise when he saw Gabe. He began to move more quickly.

Gabe followed.

Mikey and Phin gazed around the now empty alleyway.

'Where's Gabe?' asked Phin.

Lightning flashed, as Gabe scrambled across the rooftops in hot pursuit. He was gaining ground now. But L.C. knew it.

At the crest of a particularly tall building, L.C. paused, then turned and began to fling roof tiles in Gabe's direction. Gabe dived behind a chimney for cover.

'You'll never stop me,' yelled L.C. as another roof tile shattered against the chimney.

'This world belongs to me, and I'm not going to let anyone take it away!'

Smash!

Another tile shattered. Gabe winced and kept his head down. After a few moments, the smashes stopped and he risked peering out from his shelter. The roof ahead was empty. L.C. had vanished. But where?

Clang!

A noise came from the alleyway below. Gabe peered over the roof's edge just in time to see L.C. climbing through a hotel window beneath. He began to climb down after him...

'Hrrgh!'

A few streets away, Mikey grunted as he hoisted himself up onto the roof. He tried to peer through the rain.

'Can you see anything?' came a voice from below.

Mikey looked back down to see the struggling

figure of Phin, trying to climb up after him.

'Little help?' she pleaded.

Mikey sighed. He reached down and hauled her up to stand next to him. They both stared at the empty rooftops.

'Where are you, Gabe?' said Phin.

Gabe was in the dark. Quite literally.

He'd climbed in through the window and had found himself in a small hotel bedroom. It was pitch black. He tip-toed across the floor, in what he hoped was the direction of the door, treading carefully in case his foot...

Crunch!

... stood on something sharp - like it just had done.

'Hmpf!'

He clamped his hand over his mouth, desperately trying to suppress a whimper.

Too late.

'Is that you Geoffrey?'

An elderly voice quavered out from the direction of the bed.

'Er… just room service!' squealed Gabe in a panic. Then he spotted the door and dived through it, slamming it closed behind him before any more awkward questions could come up.

Now he was in a corridor. But where was L.C.? Cautiously, he crept along the hallway.

Suddenly a door opened next to him.

'Aha!' cried Gabe, and swung round towards the sound – only to be greeted by a tall, pyjama-clad man emerging from a bathroom.

Who saw Gabe...

And promptly fainted on the ground.

'Sorry,' muttered Gabe.

He carefully stepped over the man and headed onwards...

On the rooftops above, Mikey and Phin huddled together against the storm. Mikey looked at Phin. She shrugged.

'I think it's time to call in some rein-forcements,' she said.

There was a window at the end of the corridor. It overlooked a small square, on the other side of which was a tall tower. And at the top of which was perched the figure of L.C. He looked across at Gabe and grinned.

Gabe hesitated.

There was no way he was going to be able to jump across from where he was to the tower...

And by the time he climbed down the stairs to the street and then tried to climb back up again, L.C. would be long gone...

'Looks like I win,' shouted L.C.

'Actually,' said Gabe, 'you've already lost. You lost at the beginning, and you've lost again now.

'Let's face it,' he added, grinning, 'you're a bit of a loser, aren't you?'

L.C. snarled.

'Really?!' he said. 'And exactly whom do you think has got hold of your precious baby?'

'His mother,' said Gabe.

It was L.C.'s turn to hesitate.

'They're both safely tucked up back at the stable,' said Gabe. 'You didn't *really* think I'd hand him over, did you?'

L.C. looked down at the bundle he was holding in his arms.

'I'm afraid all you've got there is a bunch of straw and old rags.'

Frantically, L.C. undid the wrapping. It was indeed empty. He stared in disbelief as the straw blew away in the wind.

'You *tricked* me?!' he snarled.

'Doesn't feel very nice, does it?' grinned Gabe.

L.C. shouted back 'But I was offering you a way out... a chance to escape from the drudgery of serving God!'

'Thanks but – I'm quite happy as I am.'

'Fool!' hissed L.C. 'Well, I don't need your help anyway. I'm never going to give up. And I'm going to spend the rest of my days doing everything I can to thwart God's plans!'

'You can try. But, the thing is, your days are over. That's what I wanted to tell you. That's why I followed you. I wanted you to know that you're never going to win. You can try all you want... you can make as much noise as you want... but all your greed... selfishness... all your nastiness - it's all coming to an end. God loves this world and he's coming to reclaim his people. He's going to invade the Earth with peace and love and joy. That's what the birth of Jesus means. God is here. And he's going to win.'

In the sky above the tower, bright lights began to appear. Tiny at first, but becoming gradually brighter and bigger. It was Phin's angelic reinforcements arriving from Heaven.

Gabe smiled.

'Oh, and there's just one more thing you should know,' he called. 'I might not be any good at flying, but there is one thing I am really good at. And that's…'

He leapt into the air…

'*Crashing!*'

Gabe hurled himself in the direction of the tower. L.C. stared, open-mouthed as the little angel hurtled towards him…

Faster and faster...

Until...

Thud!

Gabe hit him square in the chest.

L.C. gasped in surprise... and then tumbled from the top of the tower down into the street far below.

Gabe skidded to a halt.

At least he tried to…

The tower roof was wet… and slippery… and, despite his best efforts, Gabe…

'Wah!'

Disappeared over the edge too…

It was a long way down.

Gabe tried not to look as he clung to the guttering just below the roof's edge, having managed to grab onto it as he fell past.

Down below him in the street, he could see L.C. picking himself up before crawling off into a sewer.

Oh well, thought Gabe, we'll get him another day.

For now, there was the rather more pressing problem of getting himself safely down from the roof.

The guttering creaked.

Gabe groaned.

But just at that moment, a head appeared over the edge above him.

It was Mikey's.

'Need a hand?' he asked with a grin.

27

Celebrations

It was much later, but still the same evening. The rain had stopped... the clouds had cleared... and the stars twinkled in the now-perfect, crystal-clear winter's night.

Gabe, Mikey and Phin wandered through the streets of Bethlehem. The residents were all now tucked up safely in their beds. However, the town was far from quiet...

Everywhere there was activity - it seemed like the whole of Heaven had arrived. There were angelic soldiers, scientists, engineers, weathermen, musicians, choristers, messengers... and a few who'd simply turned up because they didn't want to miss out on the excitement.

(Admittedly, there had been one or two raised

eyebrows when the other angels had first arrived and seen the stable, but a stern look from Mikey had put an end to too many questions.)

High above, a bright new star shone in the sky; a team of angelic engineers busily putting the finishing touches to its position.

'Made just for the occasion,' commented Phin.

'It's beautiful,' said Gabe.

The star glittered and shimmered and shone – marking for the whole world to see the place where the Son of God had been born.

Woosh!

Gabe looked around as a squad of angels took off and headed towards the hills around Bethlehem, singing songs of joy and celebration.

'I think there are going to be some very surprised shepherds in a few minutes,' grinned Mikey.

The three angels arrived back at the stable. They paused just outside the doors.

Gabe took a deep breath.

'Listen,' he said, turning to the others. 'You didn't *really* think I was going to give the baby away, did you?'

'No, no, of course not,' said Phin quickly.

'Not at all,' said Mikey.

There was a pause, then...

'Were you?' he added.

Gabe looked at his feet for a moment.

'I'll be honest,' he said, 'this whole business has been pretty tough, and I did have my doubts for a moment.'

Phin and Mikey glanced at one another.

'But,' Gabe went on, 'when I saw him there - Jesus - it changed everything. I knew that God cared. I knew that he was with us; I knew that everything was going to be okay... everything was going to be worthwhile.'

Phin grinned.

'He is pretty awesome,' she said.

'And I think, very soon,' said Mikey, 'the whole world is going to find that out too.'

The three angels smiled at each other. And with that, they opened the door and went inside the stable.

It had been a very busy night.

28

Epilogue

Some years later, there was another tree...

Actually, it was a cross...

(Although in some old writing it's referred to as a tree. I'm not sure why.

Anyway, it was made of wood...)

And there was Jesus...

No longer a baby, but a fully-grown man...

He'd been fastened to the cross, and there he'd given his life...

However, this was not an end...

Rather it was the start of a wonderful new beginning...

A new beginning that would pave the way for the whole human race to finally and truly be reunited with God the Father once more...

A new beginning that would undo all that other business with the first tree... a new beginning to bring all creation back to the way it was designed to be in the first place...

But that's another story...

ABOUT THE AUTHOR

Mike Peacock originally trained as an actor and has been telling stories to children for many years now - in schools, theatres & film. He is really pleased to be telling this one on paper.
He hopes you like it!

In his spare time Mike likes to juggle, play the guitar and teach Ju-Jitsu - although not always at the same time.

Printed in Great Britain
by Amazon